STUCK ON *You* 3

A NOVEL BY

SUNNY GIOVANNI

ACKNOWLEDGEMENTS

I have a very long list of incredible readers, yet I don't have the capacity to single you out, because I might forget someone and they might wind up mad at me over it. So, THANK YOU ALL FOR THE CONTINUED SUPPORT AND LOVE! You know you're the best. Your numbers seem to grow with each and every release, and you make me one happy author!

Porscha Sterling and Quiana Nicole, you are two hard working women that I'm lucky to work with… when I'm not pestering you for no reason at all. With each release, no matter the bumps in the road, if there are any, you two ladies smooth it out and get it done with ease. What can I say? I guess that's just what royals do.

Rooooob! Robin Conner, you have become one of my Ace Boons, and I have to say that checking my inbox every day for the last few months has been an adventure. If any normal person were to hack our accounts and tried to keep up without conversations, they would truly end up lost and scratching their heads. Thank you for being a vociferous weirdo like me. I'm not alone! Keep droppin' heat like you've been doing. I'm proud of you!

Keish Andrea and Jaimme Jaye, y'all are the truth. What I learned from you is to never judge a book by its cover, and that's only because y'all look innocent, but you keep me laughing until I'm crying. You two are amazing young women in your prime. I can see you soaring further and wallowing in your continued success. Salute!

Larissa, Misty, both Jasmines, Kendra Rainey and Shavekia, you are my A-1's. I love your honesty and your humor. Without you gals, I might have a limp in my step. Remain the goddesses you are and continue to prosper through all of the hardships and rainy days. I love you!

To my love, and the phoenix that keeps arising when everything seems to burn to ash and corrosion. (Picks up microphone to sing) Oh, and baby… I'm fist fighting with fire… Just to get close to you. Can we burn something babe? And I run for miiiiiles just to get a taaaaste! Must beee looove on the braaain! Lol! I love me some Chanel! I can't help it. It's in my veins and I come back for more dosages whenever I can. Lord, and don't I love it when you crack the whip and demand more pages and words. You've always been my good luck charm, so to come into my prime with you right here, means everything to me.

My family and distant friends, I love you. There's no disputing that. I keep you all close for a reason. That's why I praise you when I can or give you comfort. Thank you so much for all that you've done for me. You are appreciated.

SOUNDTRACK

"Happen" – **Emeli Sande**

"7 Years" – **Lukas Graham**

"Pray" – **JRY**

"Not Afraid Anymore" – **Halsey**

"Wicked Game" – **Annaca**

"Unconditionally" – **Katy Perry**

"Close" – **Nick Jonas & Tov Lo**

"Somebody" – **Emeli Sande**

"Wish You Wouldn't" – **NF**

"Now & Forever" – **Drake**

"What is Love" – **V. Bozeman**

"I Lied" – **Nicki Minaj**

"Sugarcoated" – **Justine Skye**

"Carry On (Her Letter to Him)" – **Ne-Yo**

"Answer" – **Phantogram**

PROLOGUE

Say You Won't Let Go

Miracle,

Believe me or not, I love you. I don't want you to ever think that this isn't true. Your daddy has some type of curse, demon, or witch riding his back, and it's taking everything away from him. One by one, everyone that I love is dropping and being covered in the earth. If not that, then they just leave. This includes your mother. I want to tell you how sorry I am for leaving you without getting a chance to know you. What I want you to know is that I didn't want you to be caught in the cross-fires of whatever curse this is. That's why daddy has to go. I apologize for the cowardly way that I chose, but you mean more to me than anything or anyone else on this earth, and that's without formally introducing myself. I want you to know that I tried. I tried so very hard to be a strong man and to be what everyone else expected of me. By no means do I want to lie to you or give you false hope that I'm someone that I'm not. The truth is that I don't even know who I am, Miracle. What I do know is that you're a beautiful little girl with a long and very happy life ahead of her. I wish you much peace, serenity, excellence, and success, my baby.

When you need me, just know that your stubbornness, your doggedness, and that fire in your belly is from your daddy. You truly are a miracle. Out of the womb, you proved to be stronger than I could ever be. You survived something so tragic, and that, my dear, is exactly why you're named Miracle. Somehow, if I survive this ordeal, you will be the miracle of my happiness because daddy hasn't seen much. If I don't, you know that you were made with love and that mommy and daddy love you so very much, even though we're not here.

Look for us in the stars…

De'Shane Hartford, your loving father

Xoxo

Cherie read over the letter that she snagged from the couch again. A tear fell from her eye. No matter how many times she had read it over the past few weeks, it would always hurt her and make her angry all the same. It would make her numb and halt her breathing to know that it was so easy for Shane to want to walk away from everything and everyone. She removed her cupped hand from over her mouth, wiped her cheek, then folded the letter to place it back inside her purse.

The bathroom door was gently pushed open at her side. Damon peeked in to check on her. "Baby? You okay?"

"Yes," she said with a sniffle. Cherie ran her fingers through her tresses and checked her attire in the mirror.

Damon knew better. There was something that she was keeping from him. It was something so emotional that she concealed and thought that he wouldn't catch on to it. For the last few weeks, she seemed a little more closed in and had only given him short answers.

Their fiery sex life wasn't the same either. Cherie always had an excuse as to why she couldn't join him, and she would slightly turn her head when he leaned in for a kiss. The man he was, he accepted it and tried to deal the best he could. Truthfully, he was growing weary of the fight to stick around.

Without Shane, Cherie wasn't herself. A piece of her was gone.

A cold and dismal day couldn't have had a better surrounding than that of 200 people or under, all squished together to watch the casket being lowered into the ground. The remaining five children of Apollo Cruz had heavy hearts in their chests, while their minds remained full with the memories of their late father. A single heavy breasted woman sang "Amazing Grace," and because of her pipes, there wasn't a dry eye inside of the graveyard.

Erykah sniffled with her hand over her belly. She had been holding on to a secret that only Shane knew. However, Shane wouldn't say anything about it. Because of the Lithium, Prozac, and Xanax that he was full of, De'Shane Hartford hadn't uttered a word in almost ninety days. With Erykah's fingers on her free hand intertwined with his, she could feel that he hadn't had a grip at all. Everything in their lives had shifted.

Joyce had an infant over her shoulder, and her thick lips were moving as if to be speaking to the shiny black casket with a gold trim around it. She *was* speaking. She was telling her late husband all the things that he was going to miss out on. Miracle Serenity Hartford, the three-month-old over her shoulder, wouldn't know her grandfather, and so far, she didn't know her father. Shane had seen the baby, but there was nothing that he could say to her. If only people knew what he was saying in his head, then they would indeed back off and leave him be. He was so lost in the darkness and confusion of his own brain that he had no use for a savior if any.

The only person that they all wished and hoped would pull him out of it was standing in the last row of gatherers, watching the casket like everyone else. She chewed on her bottom lip trying to contain her tears. Shane was a helpless case, and there was nothing that she could do for him. Cherie would go to see him at Tucker Pavilion and sit and talk, but she would be the only one to get a word in edgewise. She thought that he was lost. *She* lost him. Still, she would risk lunch dates with Damon to sit with him and suffer the stench of ammonia and other patients who murmured to themselves just to be there for him. She needed to find him. Joyce had given her a piece of information a few days ago that she had to gear up for, and that was the fact that the hospital was releasing Shane a week from the date. They deemed him as not being a danger to himself or others and said that he would need therapy regularly for his emotions. They would prescribe him medication, but he would have to take them as scheduled and as prescribed to keep focused.

Cherie bowed her head and thought of all that Shane had done to prove to her that he loved her, so she would have to seriously go to the ends for him, to nurse him back to mental health. Was she ready? What was she ready to give up for him? It was evident that the two would willingly die for one another, but the question was… would they *live* for one another?

CHAPTER ONE

I Know You Care

11 years ago...

"So, it's true?" Shane asked quietly. The look on his face was one of a truly heartbroken person. It was disfigured, though Cherie had yet to look into his eyes. He was at a loss. "She's not going to hold off? You're really leaving? This soon?"

"Don't say that like I want to. It's not my fault," she pleaded. "We could've done something, anything to stop this."

"How many times do I have to tell you—"

"We can do something else."

"Yeah, like what?"

"If you take my virginity before I leave, then I won't have anything to be scared over."

"Girl, you're out of your damn mind."

"No, listen. If *you* have it, then I can say that I rightfully gave it to someone deserving. You know... how they say it in sex education.

And, I would have yours. Who loves you or me more?"

"Yeah, and one day, we can totally get married, have blue collar jobs, and live in a house with a white picket fence around it and everything."

Cherie frowned at his excited expression, upset at the fact that he was basically mocking her. "I'm serious, asshole. At least we'll know that what truly belongs to us is in the right places. Nobody can steal it away from me because you'll have it. You know how you get all poetic on me and stuff? Well, think of it like you always having that piece of me that no one else can get. Maybe someone else can marry me, have sex with me, or maybe even give me a baby or two, but you will always have your own special something from your best friend."

"You do know that this is stupid, right?"

"Shane," she whined. "You said that you would do anything for me. Why go back on it now? If you don't want to just run away with me, then just do this one thing. Please?"

Though he didn't want to, Shane threw his shirt over his head and reached into his back pocket for his wallet. Thank God that the gym coach passed out condoms on a regular after class, or else he would've been screwed. To distract her, he crawled up on the bed, between her legs and laid his lips gently on top of hers. Their first kiss sent his manhood damn near poking through his boxers.

"You know, if this doesn't work, I'll still be with you, right? Not just my virginity," he told her.

"I know," she mumbled with her gorgeous eyes on his.

"You sure you want to do this?"

Cherie closed her eyes and thought of the pain that some girls spoke of during their first times, but for Shane, it would've been worth it. "Just promise me that you won't ever forget about me when this is over. When I leave, promise me that you won't replace what we have."

"I never will. I love you, girl."

Present day...

Cherie had done some digging and found that the baby would be handed off to Josiah, Jessica's father, whenever she wasn't with Joyce. On this day, she waited with Joyce until Josiah had come to retrieve Miracle. She wanted to see if she could keep Miracle for the weekend to get used to her being around before Shane was released. He was going to need to spend time with his daughter, and she wouldn't take no for an answer.

Cherie stared at a sleeping Miracle on the white plush sofa in the sitting room of the Big House. The baby was surrounded by large pillows so that she wouldn't flip over and land on the marble floors. A tear slipped from Cherie's eye. She caught it just before Joyce could walk in with herbal tea in her hand.

Joyce was wearing Apollo's golden rosaries that matched his son's in remembrance of them both. She knew what Cherie was going through. There was no use in pretending. Joyce sat the tea down on the coffee table, waited for Cherie to sit on the faint couch, then claimed the tall-back chair near the fireplace. "You ain't stopped cryin' yet, have you?"

"No," Cherie answered honestly while staring at the sleeping baby.

"I know what it feels like to look at a child that you didn't birth but was made by the man you love." Joyce daintily sipped from her small porcelain cup. "Marquita was a pretty fat baby, but it broke my heart to hear from her mama that Apollo didn't think, apparently, that I was enough for him. *Humph.* Like father like son."

"She's so beautiful." Cherie's voice wavered.

"You been by to see him?"

"A few times," she confessed, raising her cup from the glass coffee table. "He just sits there and stares into space. I think he has something that he wants to say, but he doesn't want to say it. Either that or he doesn't know *how* to say it."

"What about the house?"

"Lord." Cherie rolled her eyes before sipping her tea. Thinking of the whole ordeal made her have to take something into her body that would calm her down. It was going to take a menthol flavored cigarette, a blunt, and four cups of herbal tea to get her into a place of peace after explaining the hoops she had to jump through to claim the home that Shane had built for her. "Mama, I don't know how many times Erykah had to threaten to take her earrings off with that woman from Re/Max. We had gotten the papers saying that Shane was unable to make decisions for himself, and that took up a week and a half of our time. Then, they wanted us to pay a fee. Darius took his sweet time to respond to us in order to represent us. He gave us that sweet jive about him only being Apollo's attorney over his estate, but his estate clearly includes his children, and this is Shane's property. Good Lord. Oh, and to top it off, we have to run around Richmond to get papers notarized before the woman even gave us the keys. One problem with that."

"You need fingerprint recognition," Joyce quietly said through a laugh.

"Exactly. So, then, we had to call the security company and go through all of that hoopla all over again with them, just to get my fingerprint in the system."

"Well, I'm glad that's over. Did you get settled?"

"Not quite." Cherie huffed and sipped from her teacup. "Shane had already emptied out the kitchen and took all of his clothes out. Don't ask me where he put them—"

"The condo," Joyce interrupted her.

"The what?"

"Shane has a condo downtown. It's his own personal hideout. He probably took them there."

Cherie narrowed her eyes at Joyce. "It's like peeling a damn onion with this man. How could I have grown up with him and knew him before, and now it's like I don't know anything."

"That's what happens, baby. Boys turn to men. The sneakiness gets worse."

Cherie rolled her eyes. "At least the furniture is still there. I want to do something different to the house, though."

"Oh? Like what?"

"Well," she said with a sigh, "he built the house for me, so I want to give it back to him but in his style. He's sleek and mysterious. Shane is all about exclusiveness. He's a collector of the finer things. I think I can pull this off and make this all about him. He'll be happy when he steps foot into it."

"And the condo?"

"I think… I can pull that off too. Thank God I have a little time on my hands."

"Now, what about that man that Quita told me about? That dancer. What you gonna do with him?"

"Shit," she cursed under her breath.

"You know you can't keep him on a string, Rie. What are you going to do about him?"

"I don't know, honestly. I mean, I've seen what was out there, but Damon isn't like the rest. He's sweet and compassionate…"

"But the heart wants what it wants."

"Right," she said miserably. "Listen, I wanted to take Miracle for a day or so, just to try and get used to her before Shane came home, but I'll just wait for him so that we can learn together."

"I think that would be best. Besides, I don't think Josiah is willing to hand Miracle over to anyone else. She's given Erykah baby fever, and he won't even let her take the baby."

Cherie looked over at the angelic little one once more before she stood. There was a constant battle within herself between jealousy, envy, and being in love with little Miracle. She always thought that she and Shane would have a baby together, but she also knew that had she found her way back, then it would've been possible. Just thinking of it made her dislike her mother even more for putting her in a position to stay away from her home.

Joyce's phone rang, bringing Cherie out of her trance. She stared at the screen confusingly before she answered. "Hello?"

Cherie turned to her at the sound of the uneasiness in Joyce's voice.

"… she's standing right here, Amanda."

Cherie squinted. *What the hell was she calling Joyce for?*

"I'll relay the message."

It was Sunday, Cherie's off day. She didn't have time for shenanigans. She had to go to Ikea, give Damon some attention and narrow her list down of home décor specialists who were going to help her flip the abode that Shane had made for her. Mandy didn't speak to Cherie at Apollo's funeral, so what was it that she needed now?

"Amanda wants you to get to her house immediately," Joyce told her calmly. "Might want to brace yourself, darlin'. Some woman is screamin' in the background."

Cherie rolled her eyes, grabbed her purse from the floor, and took one last look at Miracle before she left. She couldn't wait to get the little angel all to herself, even though it still hurt to know that the baby wasn't hers.

———————

Cherie parked in the driveway of the bungalow with her eyes on the open front door. She gathered herself before leaving her car, left her purse inside, and got out to get whatever this was over with. As soon as she stepped over the threshold, she had almost tripped over the rolling luggage in her path.

"What the hell?" she whispered on the heel of a hiss.

"And you!"

Her head snapped up to see Davetta in the archway of the hall. Cherie narrowed her eyes at the woman.

"Nobody can get in touch with you, nobody knows where you are, and you're just going to vanish without even so much as telling your so called favorite cousin anything?"

"Davetta, why are you here?" Cherie sneered as she folded her arms across her blouse.

"I'm here because I don't have anywhere else to go! You would've known that had you decided to pick up a damn phone and call somebody!"

"Look—"

"No, you look! I know damn well that I ain't been the best. I know that I ain't exactly go by the motherhood handbook, but that ain't no reason to fall off the face of the earth, especially when the family needs you!"

"And when she says 'family,' she ain't talkin' about me, Rie." Mandy appeared at the side of Davetta in some sort of work uniform. It had been that long since she talked to her own cousin. Cherie didn't know that Mandy picked up a full-time job and had never missed a day or arrived late. "She's your mama, so deal with her. I'm not about to take her in to constantly hear her mouth."

"Davetta, get your shit." Cherie snapped her fingers and pointed at the luggage that she almost tripped over.

"For real?" Davetta's eyes were so wide that her orbs were the size of quarters. "It was that easy? You ain't gonna put up a fight?"

"Lady, get your stuff and come on before I change my mind."

In a hurry, Davetta pulled up her bags from the couch and the floor, then gripped the handle of the rolling luggage near the door to drag it out to Cherie's car.

"You don't have anything you want to say to me?" Mandy asked before Cherie could turn to leave.

"No," she chimed.

Mandy huffed and leaned against the pane of the archway to stare at her stubborn cousin.

Cherie left the house. She popped her trunk to help Davetta put everything inside.

"You don't know how much closer this is going to make us," Davetta commented with a grin.

"It's really not." Cherie closed the trunk and rounded the car to get in on her side. She waited for her mother to get in and close the door so that she could continue. "You're not staying with me. I have a place you can use, but you're going to have to get a job."

Davetta's jaw dropped.

"Yeah, that's right. A J-O-B. I'm not carrying your weight anymore, and that's probably why you have nowhere to go. I'm assuming because Terry's in prison and the money dried up for his lazy ass daddy. So—"

"Terry ain't in prison."

"What?" Cherie's brow raised in shock. After she went through

13

the trouble of getting him to confess and risked her own life to get it out of him, he wasn't behind bars as promised?

"Naw. Why would he be?"

Cherie opted not to say another word so that she wouldn't incriminate herself.

"Anyway, him and his daddy got into it really bad over some shit his daddy found out. Then me and his daddy had it out because he tried to take it out on me. I wasn't havin' that shit. I packed my shit and went to you and Terry's first. Terry wasn't there, but some girl helped me book a flight on his dime, and I came out here to find you."

"What... what did they get into it about?" She didn't care much for whoever her ex tried to replace her with.

"Girl, I don't know...something about investments and dodging charges. I heard Terry tell Frank that he wasn't carryin' his ass no more because his money is tied up or some shit. Who gives a fuck? My child ain't out here broke and ain't got her shit tied up. I wasn't the best mama, but the good thing to come out of that was the lesson of my girl learning to stand up on her own two feet. That's for damn sure."

"Yeah, and you're going to learn that lesson too, Davetta." Cherie pushed the start button to crank up her car. She wasn't letting her mother finesse her into paying for anything.

———————

Damon waited patiently for Cherie. He looked around the restaurant where he sat and noticed a few lovers scattered around in the bunch. The air was thick with intimacy, love, admiration and good spirits. All except for his spirit. It was drab. The woman he loved wasn't there. Even if she were sitting right in front of him, she wouldn't be there. Damon witnessed the change in Cherie months ago when she didn't speak to him for a few days. During their dinner date, she dodged his kiss. Later that night, she wouldn't even let him touch her intimately. He had a mind to ask her if there was someone else, yet he knew her to be a good girl. She wasn't having sex with anyone else. It wasn't in her body language or her speech. Once, she fell asleep beside him on the couch with her phone in her hand. He gently accepted it from her limp hand and scrolled through the messages. The only thing that caught his attention was the messages that she sent to someone named Shane before they even met. She had never mentioned someone by that name before. He noticed that Cherie only called him once before they met and none afterward. His conclusion of her not cheating was confirmed. However, Shane was the friend that she was referring to when she told him that she had to check on them. He used the texts to Erykah to cross-reference. No, she wasn't cheating, but obviously, she wasn't over him. Damon was at his end with her and the entire situation.

Finally, Cherie had arrived. Her weight dropped into the seat in front of him. She hadn't even noticed that Damon hadn't gotten up to pull her chair out for her. She whipped her straight, auburn locks over her shoulder with a smile on, yet it wiped off when she looked at the somberness on Damon's face.

"What's wrong?" she asked him.

"I love you, Cherie," he confessed with a straight face.

Her expression had become blank. This handsome man who had a stroke like no other man she had ever been with, and who had put her above all else, had knocked the wind out of her.

"The only problem is that I'm in denial."

"Ex…excuse me?"

"I try to convince myself that you feel the same way. I debate with myself very often of if you would actually say it back if I ever said it first. There's no way that you would."

"What… what would make you say that, Damon?"

"By the way you're stammering through your sentences, I know that you know that what I'm saying is true. You love Shane, whoever he is. Your heart and head are not with me, Cherie. There's no use in arguing over this. I won't do that. I also won't take you stringing me along and vice versa. In loving you and wanting what's best for you, comes setting you free."

"Damon, don't—"

"This isn't easy for me, Cherie. It's really not, but your happiness is important to me. You're no longer happy here, so I won't hold you captive. Just admit to yourself that I was a tool to help you to get over this guy. A traumatic event took place, and it made you see that it was almost too late to put whatever differences aside that you may have had to reconcile."

"But—"

"Just don't." Damon put his hands up at shoulder's length to stop her from speaking. "I would rather you not lie to either of us. And let's not forget that you're an hour and a half late for our date. That's further confirmation that your head isn't where it's supposed to be. I love you, but I can't deal. You're free to roam." He stood from his seat and pulled out his wallet to pay for the three glasses of cognac that he drank before Cherie had even arrived.

She was left sitting there in her own thoughts. This was the second time that a good man told her that she was free. She was going to have to get it together before she broke any more hearts.

CHAPTER TWO

Save Yourself From The Ruin

*F*or the past week, Cherie had trouble sleeping. She would keep herself busy by making sure that the new furniture in Shane's home was placed correctly, his wardrobe was intact, and made sure that the refrigerator was stocked. Today was the day that he would be coming home. She had sent loads of apology texts to Damon, yet she would receive no reply. Still, she pushed it to the back of her mind to make sure that the years of Shane's planning and pulling together was met within a short amount of time.

She was sitting on the barstool in front of the island when she heard the garage door raise. Cherie hopped up and rung her hands; nervousness was surely setting in.

"Together, we got plenty of power," she remembered Shane saying. This moment should've been no different.

After Shane had been pulled out of the back of the ambulance, Cherie followed. She was at his side every step of the way. The young woman stood nervously outside of the double doors of the operation room where they had to pump Shane's stomach, just to make sure that there was nothing toxic inside of him. Cherie's face was sopping wet with tears as she prayed silently that he would pull through.

Three. She counted three times that his heart stopped and the doctors went to work on getting Shane to live again. They might as well had been working on her too. Every time he flatlined, so did she. Once they had him stable and placed him in the intensive care unit, the family gathered in his room and waited for him to at least open his eyes. Because of all of the pills he swallowed that had already taken effect, Shane put himself in a comatose where he wouldn't wake for two days. Unfortunately, Erykah had already sent Cherie home to shower and to groom. Cherie received the text that Shane was able to respond to light and sound, and she shot out of the door in her pajamas and slides to get to him. When they locked eyes, there were no words to be spoken. She just didn't know that it would mean that Shane just wouldn't speak for a while.

The hatch to the door was pulled, and the first person to walk through the door was Erykah. She turned away from Cherie and stepped aside.

A size fourteen Ralph Lauren polo boot stepped over the threshold and Cherie held her breath. With his wide and tattooed hand, Shane slowly let down the hood of his designer, quarter-length shirt. When he looked up, his eyes landed on Cherie, who looked like she was about to faint. One, two steps he took to get to her and embraced her.

Cherie could've stretched out on the floor or melted inside of his arms. To feel him, to smell him, to be so close almost completed her. For a second she forgot about Damon.

When Shane pulled away, he gently kissed her forehead and moved away. He took his time to go up the stairs to his master bedroom to undress and get in the bed that he missed so desperately. Only, when he arrived, everything had changed. His bed was a white four-post canopy bed with sheer black drapes that were wrapped around each post and were ready to use whenever. The paint on his walls was white. Black "Fleur de Lis" designs were along the borders. The TV that was mounted on the wall in front of his bed was now within a black and silver picture frame, hanging as a picture would on the wall. Cherie took the style of Apollo and turned it around for his son. Everything that Shane bore witness to was his own. It was his style. He was the opposite of his father.

Shane traveled into the master bathroom where Cherie had his next outfit hanging on the wall in front of the toilet along with a pair of his new white and silver Versace pajamas neatly folded on the toilet seat. It was clear that Cherie didn't want Shane to face any more darkness. She promised him, in silence, that she would do everything in her power to make sure that it would stay that way.

He pivoted and found her reflection in the wide sink to ceiling mirror near the bed. She was turning down his thick white sheets, getting it ready for his grand relaxation session. There was a lot that needed to be said and done, but she would be damned if he had to endure anything right off. Cherie dusted off her hands and turned to the bathroom where their eyes connected. They held a stare for what seemed like hours compared to the mere seconds that it actually was.

"Why did you save me?" Shane finally spoke to break the silence.

Cherie gasped, slightly flinched, and smoothed her hands over the hips of her skirt to gather herself. To hear his voice after so long placed an extra beat in her heart.

"Rich and Rick told me. And you still hadn't talked to Mandy, yet?"

Shamefully, she looked down at the floor.

"They told me. Just because I didn't speak back doesn't mean that I don't know. Just because I was mute didn't mean that I was crazy."

"Nobody called you crazy," she mumbled.

"Look at me."

Cherie bit her bottom lip instead. Ever so slowly she made her way around the foot of the bed to leave the room. The spark that was once between she and Shane was ever so present, and it was stronger than it was before. They could feel it. Their uneven breaths proved it.

Somehow, Cherie found the strength to leave the room. Shane looked down at the floor with an uneasy feeling settling in his stomach. She was still running away from him, and he knew it.

———

Cherie entered the kitchen to fetch Shane a bottle of water. Erykah texted her earlier and let her know that they were on their way after getting Shane's new meds.

"Rie, he has to eat with these."

She turned away from the refrigerator and saw the pill bottle in Erykah's hand as she studied it.

"It's Seroquel," she continued. "I'm not sure—"

"My mama used to take Seroquel," Cherie interjected. "I know how to handle him on that. He'll basically be a zombie with a heartbeat, but I know what I'm doing."

Erykah searched through the white paper bag on the island for a moment until she found the other two pill bottles. "Why are they keeping him so medicated?"

"Because Shane had a serious disconnect from reality and they have to push him back into society at all cost. No worries, though. He won't overdose on them. I'll make sure of that."

Erykah rolled her eyes and set the pill bottles in a row on the island. "You just make sure you work your magic. My brother has to get back to work before everything my daddy left for him is shot to hell in a handbasket."

"I will, and I shall." Cherie gave her a smile before she left, and studied the pill bottle herself.

He did everything for me, she thought, *so I have to do everything for him.*

————

Shane stepped out of the shower and wrapped a towel around his waist. He reached for a shaving razor and saw that Cherie had snagged his cell phone out of the bathroom while he was bathing. There had to be a motive behind it, or else she wouldn't have just taken it. He shrugged it off and commenced to grooming. Now was not the time to let his thoughts get the better of him. They had anyway.

He thought of Apollo teaching him to shave when he was sixteen. Two weeks later, he had taken his son to the barber's to get a fresh facial and a hot towel treatment to keep his skin soft but taut. It would become a regiment for the two of them. Specifically, they would meet every Monday afternoon before work to get their straight-razor shaves and to get a little manly talk in, here and there. The only reason they stopped was because Apollo had gotten worse. They would have to call their barber over to the house. He blinked when he nicked himself with the razor. It brought him out of his memories. Quickly, he cleaned it and slapped some aftershave onto his cheeks before grabbing his outfit down from the hanger. He would save his pajamas for later. One thing his father taught him was that it didn't matter what you had going on, that if a man doesn't work, then that man doesn't eat. Mentally and emotionally drained, Shane had become king by default. There was no way that he was going to stay shut off from his kingdom when his people needed to eat.

Dressed in a white designer fleece with a red asymmetrical zipper across the torso, a pair of heavily starched white jeans, and white and red Timberlands, Shane left the bathroom and went to his new dresser to find where Cherie placed his jewelry and his colognes. After finding them, he found a white, leather wristwatch with a gold and red face on it, and a gold chain his father gifted him for his birthday that had a medallion on it in the shape of the Super Man 'S' with red diamonds filling it out. For his belt, he ventured into the closet that Cherie had left alone, except for adding a few pieces here and there and chose a red snakeskin belt that had a large gold plate for a belt buckle on it.

Finally, he pushed his head forward to whip his dreads over. Shane pulled his dreads up into a sloppy up-knot and checked his reflection in the bathroom mirror before hitting the door. Inside the kitchen, he watched Cherie intently as she swayed around it to put up selections for him that she stored inside Glad containers for him to choose from.

"I'm gone," he announced, startling her.

She whirled around to find him standing there with his keys in his hand. He slayed her entire existence with his divine smell and attire. Her words were stuck somewhere in the back of her throat.

He inched toward the island as Cherie's heartbeat escalated. His fingers coiled around one of his pill bottles, where he pulled it up to his face to read the description. Then, he unscrewed the top of it, tapped out two pills inside of his palm, and chewed them. Afterward, he grabbed his phone next to the white paper bag from the pharmacy to unlock his screen and check for messages.

"The label on the bottle says that it may cause drowsiness, so I won't be gone for long." Shane pulled on a pair of dark tinted shades and pushed them on the bridge of his nose. He gave her a smirk before turning to leave the house altogether. Today, he decided to take the tarp off of his white 1999 Chevy Monte Carlo SS. A smile appeared on his face at the beauty before him. "How long has it been, baby?" he asked the car. "Let's go to work, my love. They won't be expecting you."

It had been thirteen years since Shane drove his Chevy. Because most of the foot soldiers were used to seeing something expensive and painted in black being driven by Apollo's chauffer, Shane switched it up so that he could keep an eye on things without them knowing. He literally named the sports car "Ghost Rider." The car was junk when Erykah found it, and she bought it for $800 as a gag gift for her brother's sixteenth birthday. Unfortunately for her, his keen eye and sense of style kicked in when he saw it. He didn't see the hunk of junk that everyone else saw. He saw the finished product, and he needed it. He and Bo worked on the car for six months in between their own jobs, and even Apollo would go down to the garage of the Big House to check the progress or to make suggestions on what Shane should do to it next. Being proud of his son for practically rebuilding a whole car with his own two hands, Apollo had it taken when he sent his kids to Disneyland for spring break. He had the upholstery changed, the dashboard stripped, the shell of the radio gutted, and added on an impressive sound system for his young prince. He believed that his son deserved the best and that Shane had done more than worked for it.

When Shane slid into his Monte Carlo, on this day, he had to close his eyes and push the reason behind him no longer driving the car to the back of his mind. Just before his seventeenth birthday, he heard a song on his playlist that reminded him of Cherie, and he could've sworn that he could vividly picture her on the black and red leather seat next to him. When he shook the thought out of his mind, it was almost too late to hit his breaks. He ran a stop sign, and a Silverado t-boned him, pushing the car fifty feet away from the intersection. Shane earned three cracked ribs that day that wasn't going to heal for about three months. However, he was convinced that because the car was white was why it happened as opposed to him not paying attention to the road. Eventually, Apollo had the car fixed, but he kept the paint white, despite what his son was spewing about him being cursed.

Shane shut the door and buckled his race car styled seatbelt, and tinkered with the custom touch screen radio until he found his mp3s that he had already downloaded. Then, he tapped the top of it to have the screen of his GPS to slowly rise from the face of the flat radio. After putting in the coordinates of where he would be going, he smoothed his hands over the black leather in the seat next to him to get his aura in order. He was getting ready to live a life without his father, his girl, his mother, Ms. Pat, and it was almost too much to fathom. At least he prepared himself before he was evicted from the Pavilion. He hoped that his meds would help him in coping. He was going to need it.

Before pulling out of the garage, he connected his Bluetooth and made a call to the person who would be taking Bo's place as the right hand.

"What's up with it?" Rich answered groggily.

Shane smirked. "Man, if you don't get your punk ass up! We got to go to work! You ain't got time to be layin' all up under your chick when it's money to be grabbed."

"Now you sound like Apollo," he tiredly chuckled. "Why I didn't know you were coming home so early?"

"Probably because Erykah can't stand you and the fact that Rie still ain't talkin' to Mandy."

"That explains it. But come and scoop me, though. I'll be out front."

"Bet."

Shane decided not to wear a mask to hide his emotions or to pretend to be or do anything. He decided to live. Something that he's tried at but failed miserably. This time, he was determined not to lose. Whether it was anyone else or himself. Besides, he had to grab the remaining pieces of the ruins that were him so that he could get his daughter. He didn't want Miracle to see a failure when she looked at him. That was number one on his priority list.

CHAPTER THREE

The Comfort Of Us

Rich, sitting on the hood of Shane's car, pulled from a blunt and held it. He watched his friend go over his father's shipment one more time before he called it a day. He actually admired how Shane had everything coordinated and wouldn't miss a beat with calculations. Shane almost didn't need Rich, but Rich knew otherwise. His job was to catch what Shane might've dropped, if anything. When Shane approached the car with a grimace, Rich presented the rest of his blunt to his friend. Shane shook his head.

"Do you know that nobody been eatin' in the last month, bruh?" he harshly asked Rich.

The statement made Rich choke on what he held inside of his lungs. His droopy eyes were now wide and plastered on the warehouse in front of them.

"Shane?" Bo called him in the distance.

He whirled around and snatched off his shades. Shane's eyes were blazing with rage. "Where the fuck have you been?" he roared at his father's friend. "You explain to me right now how come it is that we got stock from last month but it ain't been dispersed!"

"I had to mourn too, Shane."

"*Mourn*?" Shane marched over to him, trying to restrain himself from backhanding his elder. "Your job ain't to fuckin' mourn, Bo! Your job is to step in when my daddy couldn't!"

"He's been buried for only a week! Been dead for two of those! You want to talk about stepping in for your daddy when you were the one who had to go into hiding! If you weren't cowering, you could've done this shit yourself!"

"*Hiding*?" Shane slapped his hand over his mouth so that he could get his words in order. He had every right to reprimand Bo for his apparent ignorance. "You know what?" he reasoned at a lower tone. "I'll give you that. Yeah, I'll let you have that. You right. His kid is supposed to uphold his legacy, and I dropped the ball. Hard, too. But you know what else? My daddy told me that everybody had to earn their keep. So, since you couldn't do your job, consider yourself on a paid leave of absence for two months."

"What?"

"Nobody worked for a month, so your punishment is to leave for twice as much. Another thing that Apollo taught me was that it didn't matter what you going through... even if you were about to bust a damn nut... you're supposed to feed the people who put money in your pocket and food on your table. He was in capacity, and so was I. That left you to work. You didn't do that. So, I'll be seeing you in two months, Bo."

Bo bit down on his bottom lip with his head tilted to the side. His friend's son had a lot of nerve to suspend him when he was there long before the boy was even in his mother's womb. "Thirty-two damn years I've been coming to his stockyard, De'Shane. *Thirty-two.* And now you want to put me in timeout because I chose to be there for my friend?"

"His wife was at his side, Bo."

"And that's supposed to make me feel better?"

"Let me ask you something, Bo." Shane folded his arms over the red zipper and stood back on his legs. "Where the fuck was I when I was thirteen, and my mother was deteriorating? Where the *fuck* was I when she took her last damn breath, huh?"

Bo took his hand across his face before he could answer. "You were here," he said miserably.

"And where I was the day before and after her funeral?"

"Picking up and dropping off money."

"So you got an excuse? Huh? She was my *mama!*"

"Shane—"

He stepped to the side and pointed over to the car where Rich sat, watching the argument, then. "You see that nigga on the hood of the car that me and you put together? Hmm? That would be my brother. Maybe not by blood, but he is. We have the same goddamn bond that you had with my daddy. But do you think that while he's struggling to breathe and is about to go that he would want me starving? I would make time to go and fuck with him and talk to him, reminisce and whatever. Afterward, I would *take my ass to work like grown men do!*"

"You won't know how it feels until it happens to you."

"But it has happened. Numerous times! Maybe my daddy didn't breed you like he did me. Or maybe you forgot what either of you taught me, Bo. You were there to watch me grow into who I am, and I won't apologize for the monster that either of you made sure that I would be. By no means do you let your best friend's legacy go to waste. No means. That motherfucker over there on that car has it understood that if I lose a hitch in my step, that he has to take that step for me. He knows that if I start coughin' up blood tomorrow, that it will be him who has to do what I would do when I'm at a doctor's appointment. Why? Because my kid ain't old enough for her to do it yet. Like I said, I'll be seeing you in two months. If I don't see you, then I understand. I'll have your replacement."

Bo narrowed his eyes at the boy he personally named the God for his flexibility, mentally and professionally, and was disgusted at the helping hand he lent to create such a being. "You're full of yourself, aren't you?"

"I was never full of myself. I just know that my daddy told me that there ain't no excuse for you not to work. Maybe I'm madder at me for taking some time off when I should've been here to get shit done. Maybe I'm mad at you for not helping me out of that dark place I was in to make sure that my daddy's shit would be right. Either way, my punishment is playing catch up while on Seroquel and Lithium, and yours is your leave of absence. Maybe Apollo Cruz should've told us both to get the fuck up and stop being bitches about our situations, but he ain't here no more." Shane casually placed his shades back up on his face and tugged at his belt buckle.

Bo sneered. "Well, all hail the new king."

Shane grimaced as his father's right-hand passed him.

He stopped at Rich and proclaimed, "Don't you let Miracle take your job away from you, Rich."

Rich dropped his head and looked at his blunt between his fingers. He had no words for the scorned older man. Everybody knew that there would be a shift when Shane came home and came to his senses, so there wasn't a reason for anybody to have a slip-up. It's just the way that Apollo built him.

"We got shit to do," Shane said as he traveled to the driver's side of the car. He waited for Rich to get in before he pulled into the warehouse and had the employees load a few bricks inside his trunk. He reminded one who his father dubbed as a Lieutenant General, right under Bo, that he would have to come back in a few hours.

Rich saw in the side mirror that other cars and SUV's were arriving. One, in particular, stood out to him. It was Shane's Hummer. It parked right next to the Monte Carlo, and out hopped Alyssa with her headscarf tied around her head and her pajama bottoms loose on the lower part of her hips. Her clinging white spaghetti strapped top beckoned for him to stare at the imprint of her bare breasts pushing against the thin fabric. Rich tried his best to remember that he had Mandy back at the house, but Alyssa's weight gain and what it had done to her body was all too tempting to resist. Shane slamming the driver's side door was the only thing to stop him from staring at Alyssa's luscious and jiggling backside. She wasn't wearing any panties, he reckoned. Thank God that Shane didn't see the way that he was almost salivating over his sister or else he would've been pissed.

"Come on!" Alyssa shouted, startling Rich in the passenger seat. Even though she wasn't speaking to him, he put his blunt out in the ashtray and got out of the car. "Y'all already been sittin' around and whatnot! Close the gate and get to packin' up!"

"Bo fucked up badly, Lyssa," Shane told her at her side. "I'm sorry about calling you on your day off. I just needed a hell of a lot of help to get this shit done and dispersed. This shit is packed up."

"Don't worry about it. Me and the girls I know will help." She folded her arms underneath her bosom as she silently counted how many bricks different men were carrying to put in the back of her brother's SUV.

"You sure they won't fold under pressure? I mean, even you. You good with being around all of this?"

"Don't patronize me, brother. I've been clean long enough to not want to go back to this shit. You just hit me from your prepaid and tell me where I'm takin' this shit."

"It's already in the GPS in my history. Just search Montgomery. It'll come right up."

"If you already know where it is, then why the hell is it in your memory?"

"Because if anything happens to me, I want Rich to know where to go and when. Speaking of which…" He checked his watch and tapped on the glass. "We're already behind by a month and thirty-four minutes. Let's get to it."

They separated to go to their vehicles when Shane stopped her. He called over the roof, "Don't let them shortchange you, either."

"Boy, please. Even though daddy was a king, I was still in the streets. I know my work." She rolled her eyes and climbed into the Hummer. She had a job to do, and nothing was going to stand in the way of that. Not even the fact that she would lose the rest of her off day to her brother's business.

Shane got into the car and buckled his seatbelt, then sent a text from his prepaid phone to his sister so that she could forward the other addresses to her friends accordingly. "Remind me to give the workers a pay raise," he mumbled to Rich in the passenger seat.

"I got you."

"And don't think I didn't see the way you were looking at Alyssa."

Rich kept his eyes forward. He had been busted in the act when he thought he was being so smooth.

"Let me remind you of what you got at home, alright?" Shane finished his text and tossed the phone into the backseat, over his shoulder. "Mandy is a good woman. Damn good one. You know this. You love her. Don't let flesh come between you and her when y'all are finally official and in a happy place. Even if you're not in some type of paradise, I'm sure that it ain't somethin' that can't be fixed. Alyssa London is a recovering addict. Beyond that, she's a Cruz woman. Came from my daddy's sack just like the rest of us. She ain't dainty like Mandy, and she ain't gonna take you comin' in the house whenever you want to run the streets with me. Other than that, Alyssa London is my sister, Rich. My *sister*. If you touch her... I will do you harm."

Rich looked over at Shane to search through his eyes for a second. When he found that his friend was being completely honest, he faced forward again and said, "Alyssa been off limits. I just couldn't help the fact that she's juicy now." Slowly, a smile crept across his face.

Shane dropped his head and chuckled. "If anything, I thought you would've gone after Erykah."

"Hell naw. Erykah would fuck me up. That mouth on her is a motherfucker."

"Tell me about it." Carefully, Shane backed out of the warehouse and waited for the employees to close the rolling doors before he pulled off. He was no stranger to a hectic situation. He was the king of fixing issues within Apollo's operation. Today, however, he had a long list of things he needed to accomplish before he could even lay his head on his pillow.

———

After a long day, Shane finally returned home after showing his face to many people since he had his stay at the Pavilion. He dropped his two duffle bags of money in his study, shut the light off whilst reminding himself to double count it in the morning, and traveled up to his bedroom.

From the bed, Cherie could hear Shane softly speaking gibberish. She leaned up, wondering what the hell he was saying and who it was he was talking to. Unfortunately for her, she had the sheer drapes let down around the bed so she wouldn't have been able to see him until he pulled them apart in the dark room.

"You know I love you, right?" he murmured. Cherie's eyebrows squeezed. She just knew that he didn't bring some floozy into the home that she remade for him. "There is nobody on this earth more special than you. I don't care how long I've known them, how much I've done for them, or how many times I've said that I loved them. You are my one and only." Cherie could hear him give this woman a kiss.

That's when she had had enough. She was going to mess them both up for walking into their home and for having the audacity to forget all about her. She angrily pulled apart the drapes and touched the side of the lamp on the nightstand to illuminate the room. What she saw made her feel more than foolish.

Shane stopped just shy of his dresser and turned to see her there in her silk, silver nightie. They stared at one another like deer caught in headlights until Shane was able to break the silence.

"What… what are you still doing here?" he asked nervously.

"I should be asking you why you're coming home late… and with her." She pointed weakly at the limp baby that Shane had propped on his arm with her sleepy head resting against his shoulder.

"She's my kid," he shot back with a hiss and disgust on his face.

"No, no. Not like that. Shane, do you know what time it is?" Cherie traveled around the foot of the bed and stopped shy a few steps away from him and little Miracle. "Don't tell me you went over to Josiah's and woke her up, just to bring her home with you. You'll get her sleep schedule off balance like that. She just made it over three and a half months. You don't want to knock her off track."

"Rie, I got this," he quietly chuckled as he made his way over to his closet. He took the black diaper bag off his shoulder and dropped it, then used the heel of his boot to slide the door closed. "Just because I was in an institution, it didn't mean that I didn't read. I read up on things that I was going to have to do for her. I never really stopped to ask myself why a house for crazy people had baby magazines in the library, but they did." He took his time to take her over to his bed, parted the drapes with his elbows, and laid Miracle on the soft sheets. "When Mama J came to visit, she would keep me posted on how big she was getting, and she gave me advice on how to take care of her. And it's crazy because... she's the only thing that is proof on this planet that I'm not crazy and that I don't get to lose anymore. I gained an unconditional love."

Cherie stared at him for a moment. She was a little slighted because of his statement. Still, she understood where he was coming from.

Shane turned to her. "What?"

"She's... just so beautiful."

"Listen, Rie, I'm sorry. I didn't know that Jessie was pregnant until you were already gone. I should've reached out to you and told you, but I thought that you were still mad at me. I thought that you were going to somehow choose Terry over me, and I couldn't face that. So, I left you alone and kept an eye on you just to make sure that he wouldn't try nothin' with you like putting his hands on you again. I tried to make something work with Jessica, only because I tried to replace you and distract myself."

"Shane, don't say that."

"It's true. I was honest with myself and hurt myself for three months over it. I'm sure me saying it aloud won't be any less of the truth. I can tell you one thing, though. It hurts a hell of a lot less than it did when I was in a room with pillows for walls, staring at a ceramic tile ceiling. Now that I've told the truth out loud, I'm just ready to put the past behind me. What about you?"

"Can I...? Can I have my best friend back?" she inquired with nervousness rattling her bones at the answer as she awaited it.

"Is that what you want, Rie?" he grumbled, taking another step closer to her.

"Yes," she responded softly.

"Good. I can give that to you. Right now, though, I have to get in the shower and get ready for bed. I have to do this shit all over again tomorrow and the day after that. You wouldn't believe the shit that happened."

Cherie fluffed her hair, leaning against the post on the bed. "Well... I'm sure you're going to tell me about it, love."

"Sho. Now come to the shower so that we won't wake Miracle up."

Cherie bit her bottom lip and followed behind her friend while he stripped. She listened to his whole spill about what was going on with the business and was almost shocked that he let Alyssa in on it. Still, she sat there on the toilet and listened to him over the roaring waters. Shane was a serious motor-mouth tonight. It took her back to when her friend wasn't all secretive and mysterious. He was her Shane again. He could talk her to sleep and make her laugh at the drop of a dime. Three or four times, she laughed so hard that she had to shut it off and peek into the room to make sure that Miracle was asleep. And when it was bedtime, Cherie laid on one side of Miracle with the little one's father on the other side.

Shane stared at her through bedroom eyes and bit the corner of his bottom lip. He wanted badly to tell her that he loved her, but he couldn't. He figured that it was too soon and that he didn't want her to act like a frighten kitten and run away from him. Shane reached over his sleeping daughter and stroked Cherie's arm lovingly to sooth her. He knew that every time she looked at Miracle, it would remind her of how she hadn't been the one to take his seed.

Cherie, on the other hand, tried her best not to doze off. There were things that she wanted to tell him too, but she wouldn't dare to open up about them just yet. Shane had just gotten home, and even though she knew that it was dangerous for him to get back to work so soon, she didn't want to put any more pressure on him.

"This feels good," Shane grumbled with his eyes closed.

"What? Your Seroquel taking effect?"

"No, crazy little woman," he chuckled. "Us."

CHAPTER FOUR

Trouble Ahead

Cherie rode with Shane to take Miracle to Josiah. She wanted to have a word with him, but she decided against it. She wanted so badly to ask him where he knew her from. Shane jogged out of the two-story colonial home and hopped inside his Jaguar. He took the Baby on Board sticker out of the back window, then started the car. Cherie clamped her thumbnail between her teeth. She sat quietly while looking out of the passenger window.

"What's wrong?" Shane asked. He pulled away from the curb and fondly rested his arm against the armrest. Secretly, his fingers were itching to touch hers.

"Nothing," she lied.

"Rie, come on. Don't do that. It's me. You can talk to me."

"It's nothing. Really."

"Okay. Then what's it going to take to make you happy, huh? I mean, you act like I don't see the sadness in your eyes. I know it's there. Do I need to remind you of how much I know you? Girl, I could write a stock of books on how well I know you. Spill it."

"It's not the right time," she mumbled.

"Any time is the right time, but I don't want to push you into anything."

"She's just so beautiful," she then admitted quietly.

Shane's head snapped toward her at that moment. Luckily, he was slowly stopping at a red light. "Who? Miracle?"

"Yes." Cherie's eyes welled.

"Come on, Rie. Talk to me. Tell me what the matter is."

"Shane… I had an abortion."

Even though the light turned green, Shane didn't go. He couldn't take his eyes off of her at her confession.

"I was seventeen and was just hollow after all the shit that I had been through because of my mama. Then… we wind up in California and the next thing I know, I'm engaged. You want to know why?"

Shane gulped as opposed to answering. He was afraid of hearing the truth after so long.

"I was living a damn lie. I thought that I could somehow take control of my life, and I was living recklessly. So reckless, that I let a man beat on me without so much as fighting back. Coming back to Virginia would've been the worst mistake ever because I thought that if I did, I would only be living a fantasy. I didn't think that things between us would've been the same. I thought that they would've been forced or either I would've run into you being with another woman. I don't know what's wrong with me."

Suddenly, Shane's head tilted back, and a smile appeared on his face.

"What?"

He let out a shoulder-shaking laugh at her, but Cherie didn't find it funny at all.

"What the fuck is so funny, De'Shane?"

"I felt the same way!" His laugh grew louder and louder, yet all Cherie could do was fold her arms and watch with a raised brow. "Swear to God... me and Jessica went out on a first date, simply because from a distance, she looked like you! And the one reason that I continued to date her was because I tried replacing you. I mean, naw, it didn't work, but that shit's crazy right? Even without each other, we were still trying to find our footing and kept trying to replace each other."

"I damn sure do hope that it's your meds that have you laughing so damn hard."

"No... it's the fact that we should've said this a long time ago. What were we thinking? Yeah, so it's cool not to open up to one another because we don't know each other?"

Finally, the two paid attention to the honking horns behind them. Cherie rolled her eyes and sank into her seat as Shane went through the light.

"Seriously, though, Rie," he sniffled, trying to get himself together. "We should've sat down a while ago to talk shit out like adults. As far as the abortion, how come you didn't tell me?"

"What was I supposed to say, exactly?"

"I don't know, but you knew that I would've listened."

"Shane, I'm just now getting you back. The you that I remember anyway, and it took a nervous breakdown, months in an institution, and antipsychotics just to bring you back to me."

"Still, we can talk about it another time. I know that things seem glum now, but they won't be. You know why?"

"Because together, we got plenty of power?"

A smile reappeared onto his face. He reached over and grabbed Cherie's hand to clasp their fingers together on the armrest.

———————

Almost twenty minutes into their drive, and Shane pulled into a parking space on the side of his sister's shop that she basically named after her and her siblings. Royal Six's was amply named because they all considered themselves as royalty. It had been a while since Shane had actually entered the building, so instead of dropping Cherie off, he walked her in. The gentleman he was, he opened the door for her and didn't stop her when she scurried to the back to get ready for work.

He approached the counter and looked through the selection that his sister made with her own two hands. A flurry of emotions hit him at once. He bought Jessica's bracelet that somehow kept falling off her wrist from there. It wasn't until she bought a clasp from Wal-Mart and replaced the original that a link broke off it and she had to have Erykah to fix it before she died. Then there was the feeling of joy when he thought of ordering he and Cherie's necklace and bracelet set.

"Hey, brother," Erykah greeted him groggily.

He looked up and saw her, with a smile instantly appearing on his face.

Erykah had to stop in mid-step to look at him strangely. Her brother never smiled as wide or big before.

"You know I need a piece from you," he stated.

"Why are you in such a good mood?"

"I don't know," he chuckled. "Life, I guess."

"Life, huh? Or did you take a dip inside the Cherie Caves?"

"I resent that!" Cherie squealed as she swayed out of the back room and over to the counter. "Anyway, De'Shane. Are you going to buy something? We have to get started."

"Yeah, I'm going to buy something, but I'm just going to come back later."

"Have a good day."

He winked at Cherie and threw a salute at his sister before leaving. Cherie watched him leave, savoring the scent of his cologne while it lingered in the air. Erykah could tell that something was on Cherie's mind that she was trying to hide. She was an easy book, even though she thought that she wasn't.

When Erykah saw Shane's car pass the double doors of the shop, she sat on her stool to have a good talking with the young woman. She pulled her long braids behind her back and stared at Cherie.

"What?" Cherie giggled.

"You still love him, don't you?"

"You know I do, so I don't even understand why you're asking."

"Because there's something between y'all—"

"I know." She crossed over Erykah to stare at the new pieces that her friend and boss put on display so that she could familiarize herself with them.

"Listen." Erykah huffed and stood, hoping that Cherie wouldn't notice the small pudge pressing against the puffy fabric of her high-waist skirt. "There's an opportunity in California, and I can't fly for reasons that I'm not at liberty to discuss at the moment."

Finally, Cherie looked over at her through a squint.

"Since you're very accustomed to the rich and snotty in Cali, I figured that you can take my place. I trust your judgment."

"What opportunity?"

"There's a guy out there who has a shop that was struggling. He's going bankrupt. He wants to get rid of the pieces he has, and he wants to sell me his place. Now I'm not telling you to run the place, I just want you to help him sell the remaining pieces and tell me about the building. You have a good eye, so that's why I said I trust your judgment."

"Okay, well I can call some of my old friends and get them to open some of their husband's wallets. It's no problem. How do you think over half your stock keeps flying out of the cases? I've been putting them on Instagram. As soon as they're bought through the website, I ship them off."

"Smart little wench."

"Of course," Cherie smirked and shrugged.

"It'll be two weeks from now, though. I hate last minute shit, and

I guess that's why he's in this bind now."

"Relax. It gives me enough time to work my magic."

"Good."

"What's wrong, though? Are you okay, Erykah?"

She ignored the concern in Cherie's eyes and put a smile on her face. "Of course I'm okay. Oh! I almost forgot!" she snapped her fingers and looked at the clock. "You won't be here today. You got an appointment at Quita's in twenty minutes."

"Shit!" Cherie palmed her forehead as she whirled around to the clock on the wall. "I almost forgot too. Worried about Shane and having him comfortable by the time he got home threw me off track."

"Well, you better get going."

"Shane dropped me off," she whined.

Erykah rolled her eyes and traveled into the office. "And this is exactly why I don't let niggas drive me places." She grabbed her keys out of her purse and dangled them in front of Cherie's face when she returned. "Bring my baby back in one piece, and stop by KFC on your way back...or else, I swear to God that you're not my sister-in-law, I don't know you, and you're fired. Don't even look for a W-2 in the mail, bitch, because you forgot my damn KFC five-dollar fill-up box."

"Fine," she laughed as she accepted the car keys.

After work, Shane drove around Richmond until he arrived at the RAMZ Apartments, for the University of Richmond students. It was surprising to him that Ashington was able to live in such luxury, or would be able to afford it with the allowance that their father was giving her. She was up to something, and he needed to find out what that was.

He parked on the street and found the door number that Alyssa had given him the day before. When he reached the door, loud music was blasting, but that wasn't what caught his attention. Not even the fact that the voice over the music was his sister singing on the track. It was the yellow slip of paper that was tacked on the door, staring him the face, telling him that this was Ashington's second warning. Shane narrowed his eyes as his infamous grimace flooded his face. His left eye twitched. His head began to pang as a side-effect of the Lithium that he had taken hours prior. Shane snatched the paper off the door and took his wallet out of his back pocket. From the folds, he pulled out what looked like a long silver pin, and another with a hook on the end of it. He didn't want to knock. He wanted to catch Ash in the act of whatever the hell she was doing. It was already fishy that she hadn't given anybody a key to her new place.

Successfully picking the lock, he entered without so much as calling her name or skipping a step in his walk. He could smell weed in the air. Shane's eyes might as well had blazed a bright red when not thinking that maybe Ash had a roommate that could've been a stoner. He lifted his nose heavenward to detect the second scent in the air. His heartbeat was escalating, and the Lithium made him see stars. His medication was warning him to calm down before something worse could happen to his brain or body, yet Shane didn't listen to it.

He marched into the hallway and found a closed door. Without caring who was behind it, he kicked it off the hinges and stormed through.

The lovers under the covers flinched at the sound of the bang Shane made with the bottom of his Nike boot colliding with the wooden door, and the young man that was on top turned to see the mammoth charging for him. He didn't have time to save himself. Shane grabbed him by the back of the neck and slung him into the wall, just as Ash shrieked, trying to cover herself.

"You out of your goddamn mind?" Shane yelled at her.

"Brother, when did you—"

"Put some fuckin' clothes on!"

Ashington quickly covered herself and ran into her walk-in closet to dress.

"And who the fuck are you?" he screamed at the naked young man, who had yet to gather himself or realize what was going on. "Who are you, nigga? You got my sister smokin' weed?" Shane grabbed the burning blunt out of the ashtray and flicked it onto the young one's manhood. He held him by the throat to keep him from getting off the floor, ignoring his screaming, then kneeled beside him to stare into his eyes. "When I let you go, you get your ass out of here and as far away from my sister as possible."

As soon as Shane let him go, the boy hopped up from the floor, found his clothes and shot out of the bedroom with them all wadded in his arms. Shane grabbed at his skull to keep his headache at bay. Ashington was in big damn trouble for what she had going on in her apartment.

"Get your ass out here!" he loudly demanded.

Shyly, dressed in a long t-shirt and leggings, Ash tiptoed out of the closet with her head down.

"You're out of your motherfuckin' mind, Ash!" Shane raved as he snatched the remaining sheets of the bed. He was so angry that he was tossing them around the room. "You're smoking weed, too? No wonder you were always calling to get Erykah off your ass when she had every damn right to put her foot up your ass and through to your esophagus. You fuckin' now? Unprotected? What the fuck is wrong with you?"

"Brother—"

"Put them goddamn sheets in the laundry basket before I set this fuckin' room ablaze!"

Ashington hopped to. There was no time to waste while Shane that God was on your ass.

"Who was that nigga? Did you even know him? I ain't heard shit about you having no boyfriend!"

"He was just a fr—"

"Turn that *goddamn* music off!"

Ashington flinched at her brother's command, but she did what she was told.

Shane paced the room with his hands on his hips so that he could calm down. He was a father now, so he had to think like he would if Miracle was caught in college, in this situation.

When Ashington returned with a bowed head, she was met with a thunderous sound and blazing hot pain shooting up her leg. She screamed and backed away from her belt-wielding brother. He didn't just stand there and let her get away either. Shane followed her into the living room area while swinging his black, snakeskin belt. Each time he connected with her legs, yet the thin fabric of her leggings wasn't helping to ease the pain. He ignored her screams, cries, and pleas for him to stop. She had to learn her lesson one way or the other. Finally, on her back with her feet up, she grabbed the belt and held on to it for dear life.

"Let go of my shit, girl," he warned her through closed teeth.

"No!" she cried. "You're just going to hit me again!"

"You are goddamn right I'm going to hit you again. Now, let it the fuck go."

"You can't do this to me! I'm a grown woman!"

"Grown my ass! I don't give a fuck how old you get! You are *my* little sister, and you ain't gonna run around here like some little tramp ass bitch. Now let my belt go, Ash!"

"No!"

"Alright," he said calmly, and let the belt go.

Ash fell on her back and scooted away from him.

Shane wrapped his dreads into a tight ball behind his back as he marched over to her and punched arm and her thigh.

"Stooop!" she screamed, trying to kick her brother off.

"So, you just gon' come out here and make us all look bad? Like this is what we do?" Shane was seething. "You randomly fuckin' niggas now?" He hit her again in her thigh, and with force. "You out your fuckin' mind."

Before he could hit her again, the front door swung open. Her Caucasian roommate stepped through in shock when seeing her friend getting hit in the leg like she was a grown man off the street.

"Fuck you want?" Shane asked her angrily.

"Umm… is this some sort of nasty role-play thing?" she asked nervously.

"What? Man, I'm her *brother*! Get the fuck out of her until she calls you and tells you that it's okay to come back! Fuck outta here!"

Without any other word, her roommate stepped outside and shut the door behind her.

"You're not supposed to hit girls!" Ashington screamed.

"You ain't a girl, you're my kin. Now get your stupid ass up."

In pain and all, Ash stood and straightened her disheveled hair. "Brother, please don't tell Er—"

"Don't tell Erykah?" he sarcastically asked her. "Oh, don't tell? Girl, like I said, you're out of your goddamn mind. Not only am I going to tell her, but you're going to live with her."

"Shane!"

"How the fuck do you even afford this place, huh?"

"I can't really afford it unless I—"

"You know what? I don't even want to know." He put his hand up and turned away from her. "I can't believe you. I didn't expect none of this shit from you."

"Shane, I'm sorry—"

"Do you not know what the hell I have had to go through to get to this point?" Shane whirled around to her with his anger subsiding. "Girl, I've been through hell and back, and I'm still almost done with my masters. Had it not been for internet connection at the Pavilion and computers in the library, then I wouldn't have been able to keep up with my lectures. Oh, but you can sit around here and fuck with niggas and smoke weed. Okay." Shane pulled his phone from his back pocket to put his sisters in a conference call.

"What are you doing?" Ash panicked.

"Fuck it look like? Puttin' your sisters on a conference call."

Ashington's life might as well had been over.

CHAPTER FIVE

Sleeping With The One I Love

"Quita, call Rick," Shane prompted her.

"Don't do this!" Ashington pleaded.

"What's up, Quita?" Erykah greeted her sister.

"Rick, call Lyssa," Shane demanded.

"What's going on?"

"Don't ask questions. Just do it."

Quickly, she phoned the last sibling and waited until Alyssa answered. Shane spilled everything from the weed to the unprotected sex and the second to the last warning before eviction. He ignored Ashington screaming in the background of how he had abused her, and continued on his rant. He wasn't taking that shit from her. He was serious when he said that she was going to live with Erykah. She was the only one who was going to swing the iron fist as their father would. He would be damned if her future went down the drain because of her foolishness.

––––––––––

Cherie closed the shop for lunch and went to the bar up the street for a drink. She didn't expect for her bartender to be Damon, though it was. He was the only one working the shift. When he asked what she would like, she looked up at him in shock. She was so busy replying to the responses she had gotten from her mass text about organizing a jewelry party, that she didn't notice him wiping down the counters. Because of her reddish brown pixie cut, he barely even recognized her. They both looked on at one another in shock.

Damon cleared his throat and popped his neck. "Mango margarita?" he quizzed.

"Sure." She slapped a fake smile on and took her attention back to the phone in her hand.

Shortly, he returned with her drink and sat it in front of her. Moments later, they were stored in the stock room with Cherie on the small table at the back. Her legs were over Damon's shoulder, and his face was shoved between her legs. The only thing that made her push him away was not the orgasm that was vastly approaching. It was the blare of Shane's ringtone that she set earlier in the morning.

"*Oh, I pray... I know that I've been cruel. Oh, I pray! I know not what I do!*" "Pray" by JRY and Rooty blasted from her purse, and guilt sank in. "*I pray for peace. Tell me why don't you?*"

The entire song itself was so reminiscent of her Shane that it was ridiculous. It was the only reason she set the tone in the first place.

"*I want to throw it all away for tonight and to die another day. It's just you and me, and I'm on my knees. Would you pray for me? Would you pray?"*

When the synth of the chorus sounded, Cherie knew that she was in trouble. She pushed Damon once more to successfully move him away from her.

"I'll call you," she said as she adjusted the seat of her panties before scurrying away.

He was left standing there, in awe at how she could be brought out of ecstasy so quickly.

———

Cherie contacted Erykah to let her know that Shane had called and that she closed the shop an hour early to get to him. Luckily for her, Erykah understood that when Shane barks, you had better hop to. She parked on the street, in front of the house, and bolted inside and up the steps. She then dropped her purse on the side of the bed and placed her cell phone on the nightstand. After taking her heels off, she went to find Shane in the room that she converted into Miracle's. She was surprised to see that he was actually using it.

Lightly, he bounced her on his forearm to get her to settle down a little.

"What happened?" she asked with worry in her voice.

"It's okay, baby," Shane told Miracle, with his eyes shut. "It's not going to be so hot anymore in a little while. It's going to go away, my little mama."

"Shane?" Cherie inched into the room a little more to see the real tears glossing Miracle's miraculously entrancing brown eyes that had a twinge of gold in them, like her father's. She lay limply against her father's chest with two fingers inside her mouth. Her chunky face was so darling, but her cheeks were rosy red, and so was her little nose. Cherie had to lay her hand on her chest as if the wind had been knocked out of her. "What happened to Miracle, Shane?"

He waited until Miracle's eyes drooped and she had finally let the infant's Motrin take effect before he gently laid her in her crib. Then, he went back to his room and shut the doors behind Cherie.

"Where the fuck was you?" he asked her angrily. "I called you as soon as I was told that I was going to have to get her from daycare. You know how long it takes you to go to Wal-Mart and look through meds to find what you're looking for? Hell, even Josiah couldn't get out of work because he had a patient who had a botched job, and the patient was on the table at the time."

"Shane, I'm sorry. I had to take inventory and whatnot before I could close up for the day. Even Erykah is understanding of that."

"You should've been there. I was scared out of my damn mind, and I called you without you being there when you needed to be."

"I don't even know what happened!"

"Of course you wouldn't because you didn't answer the damn phone! You were on break, Cherie!"

"Wait... how do you know when my breaks are?"

"Because I called Erykah to verify so that I could surprise you. Unfortunately, I was called away about my daughter."

"Surprise me?"

"Nice hair, by the way." Shane crossed over her and sat on the foot of the bed with a panging head. His meds were warning him again to keep as calm as possible, but he was ignoring them yet again.

"Quita did it," she mumbled.

"Yeah, I know. Just like I know that after you had left there, you went back to work for all of an hour before your break."

"Why are you being so mean to me, Shane? I'm here now! That's what's important."

"What's important is you telling me why it is that you didn't even so much as call me back! Anything at all could've been happening, and you chose work over whatever it could've been."

"That's not fair."

"Oh, but it is. Anytime you've needed me, I've dropped whatever the fuck it is that I was doing to get to you. Yet you haven't reciprocated that. Is it going to be that way, Cherie? Because, if it is, you might as well just get your shit and walk out of here."

"Can we just stop arguing?"

"You are so unbelievable." Shane shook his head.

"How, Shane? Now you have no excuse. I've done everything you've done for me. So, what now? What can you possibly say that will make me look—"

He stood and eyed her for a second. Strongly, his hands latched onto Cherie's jaws and his lips powerfully connected with his hers. He backed her toward the bed while removing their tops. Cherie knew that she should've stopped and thought of Damon, but how could she with Shane's aggressiveness that she missed so much?

"I need you here," he grumbled against her lips. "You can't just leave me hanging no more, especially when I have a whole other person who's going to need you as well."

As soon as they landed on the made bed, and Shane adjusted himself between Cherie's legs, Miracle let off like a siren to make them both remember that she was there and that she most likely needed to be changed.

Both of them shut their eyes tight, feeling guilty that, they forgot that Shane's daughter was in the home for a second.

"I'll get her." Shane left Cherie on the bed to retrieve Miracle.

Cherie waited until he was out of the room to fetch her phone from the nightstand to check her messages.

Shane shot back in the room with a strange brown substance on his abs. She didn't have time to see what it could've been, but she could've guessed when he complained from the master's bath. "Can you go and wrap that up? That was projectile. For real, for real."

She rolled her eyes with a small smile on her face, then eased her way out of bed to clean up whatever mess Miracle could've made. Shane finished washing off his abs and went back into the bedroom to find a shirt that he could pull on when Cherie's vibrated across the nightstand. He narrowed his eyes at it, trying to figure out why her phone was on vibrate, to begin with. He ventured over to it and looked down at the name on the screen and the heart-shaped eye emojis that surrounded it. Shane's blood boiled at the message just underneath it.

"Baby, I'm worried. Please call me. Is everything alright?"

Shane picked up the phone and clicked on the message. He scrolled through the thread to see many things that he wasn't supposed to. Even Cherie's nude photos that she sent to this Damon person. His nostrils flared at Damon telling Cherie that he loved her. He did notice, however, the fact that Cherie never said it back. What almost sent him over the edge were the millions of apologies that Cherie sent to Damon. She was practically begging for this man to speak to her.

"All done," she sang as she strutted into the room as if she had accomplished something that was supposed to be more than difficult. Her smile faded when she saw Shane's frown. "What's wrong?"

I'm not worthy, he told himself. I won't ever be enough. I'm not who she wants or needs. Drop that shit and let it go. Yeah, it would've been a beautiful happily ever after that would make a lot of people tear up because two best friends grew up in love and married, but that's all it's ever going to be. Just a damn fantasy. You're a grown ass man, De'Shane. You're a king with a princess, and it's time that you start acting like one. You didn't go away to get yourself together or come home to take nasty ass pills that fuck with your emotions, for Cherie. You did that shit for Miracle. She's the only woman that counts anyway. Take your time to get over it before you fuck around and strangle this bitch.

"Shane, you're scaring me. What's wrong?"

From the other side of his leg, Shane pulled her phone up and casually handed it over to her. "Damon wants to know if you're okay because he's worried about you. I replied on your behalf and told him that you were. I even told him that you were going to call him back.

You might want to get that taken care of." He rose from the bed and left his room. Shane wanted badly to slam his doors behind him, but he gently closed them instead to give Cherie some privacy.

She stood there in shock, ready to relieve her bladder all over the hardwood floors at what had just taken place.

Shane went into Miracle's room and grabbed her out of her crib with a smile on his face. "You're so chunky," he teased her. Easily, he sat in the rocking chair that Cherie stylishly placed beside the crib, and cradled her in his arms. He rocked in the chair while staring down at her little angelic face and marveled at her caramel complexion. "I swear I love you," he told her. "You have no idea how this whole love thing works yet. Well… I don't think any of us understand it, but what we do know is that you can't help who you love. And daddy loves his baby. I just wish that I was there before this, to see you get to this point."

Miracle reached up and grabbed Shane's nose. In turn, he kissed her palm.

"Hey, I think we got to get some more fluids in you. At least your fever is breaking, right? Another incident like that and daddy's going to have to take you to the ER for sure. I don't want anything ever happening to you."

A tear slipped from Cherie's eye at how he sounded so gentle and happy with his daughter. She tiptoed out of the master bedroom and stood outside the nursery shortly after Shane had closed the doors. She didn't know what she was doing wrong, but she was going to have to figure it out if she wanted to be a part of the family that he created.

Shane rocked with Miracle while giving her diluted Gatorade that he had made before Cherie had even arrived, and even he fell asleep the same as she had.

CHAPTER SIX

It's Always Been There

"Still can't believe it," Shane said as he placed the last poster on the wall of Rich's new man cave.

"What's there not to believe?" Rich responded. He plopped down inside his recliner and crossed his ankle over the opposite knee.

"You and Mandy, bruh. Y'all were cool as fuck together. What happened?"

Rich waited for Shane to take a seat in the recliner across from him before he explained the best he could. "It must be in the bloodline or something because Mandy was out of her damn mind. Every time I turned around, she was accusing me of cheating."

"Well?"

"Ain't no *well*. I was faithful to that woman, and any other woman that has tried to come on to me could tell her that. When she told me to pull my dick out so she could smell it, I started looking for houses on Craig's List. Do you know how it feels to deal with our kind of work, then come home to yelling, screaming, accusations, and having somebody to talk down to you like you're less than who you really are?"

"Nah. I can't say that I do, bruh."

"Well, good. It ain't a good feeling. I just kept shit on the low because as soon as she gets in from work in the morning, she'll be pissed as fuck to see all my shit gone."

"What?" Shane chorused.

"I had the movers take all my shit out as is. I packed what I could while they were grabbing shit. Started as soon as she hit the door at five this morning. Had my furniture delivered on time too."

"Why didn't you tell me?"

"Because I didn't want you to try and talk me out of it, Shane. I loved that woman with everything I had, but it wasn't enough for her."

"Damn." Shane pushed his back into the soft upholstery of the recliner with his eyes heavenward. "I know that feeling. To be under-appreciated. Or... as they call it... showing their love in a different way."

"That's exactly what she said last night. Talkin' 'bout how she shows her love in a different way. Shit, just the other day, she stayed out all night and didn't come home at all. Then, when she tiptoes in the house at eight the next morning, she's giggling and shit on the phone. I ain't up for them damn games. Now you see why I'm in my own place."

"I don't blame you."

"Speaking of which, I'm having a house party next week—"

"Nigga, you were really planning shit, weren't you? All the way on the low."

"I was. I want you to be there."

"Oh, nah. You know I got to get Miracle."

"Shane, that ain't no request."

"Fine," he stated, shaking his head. "You just better make sure that it's worth it."

"Oh, but it will be."

———

A week had gone by, and Cherie and Shane only coexisted. Three days ago, she was tired of missing him in the morning. He would fall asleep in Miracle's nursery, sleep in the spare room, and then he was up at God knows what hour just to take his daughter to daycare. He would give her short answers to her texts, and wouldn't be home for dinner. It was apparent that Shane was avoiding her at all cost, maybe to keep some of his words to himself. Today, however, she knew that he had a much-needed appointment with Quita, and she planned to stop by.

After having her flight and reservation for her event set at an old friend's home in California, she received the confirmation text for her hotel room and one from Quita that told her that Shane was almost done drying.

She locked up the shop and got into her car, pushing the feeling of fear to the back of her mind. They needed to talk, and they needed to set some boundaries.

As soon as she parked on the side of the building and had gotten out, she rounded the corner and almost bumped into him. She lightly gasped and took a step back. Shane, on the other hand, kept walking.

"Wait," she called, keeping up with his stride that wasn't at all quick.

"Shane, we need to talk."

"We don't have anything to talk about," he returned, just above a whisper. He snatched open the door to the Hummer and took a step up to get inside it.

"We do, and we need to do it now."

"Okay. Let's talk." He got out and close the door, staring directly at her. "You don't love me like I love you, Cherie."

"What?" she asked with a hiss.

"You don't belong to me. You're not my property. Whereas I go to the edges for you, you don't. Not a drop of thought or consideration anywhere."

"I redid your entire house!"

"It was supposed to be *our* house! Where's your style in there? Huh? I don't like white. Anybody could've told you that. Had you known me like I know you, they would've told you that I like gray, red and black. But nobody has to tell me what Cherie likes. You even like to quiz me on things you like, and I aced those bitches every time you used to. What pisses me off about you is that you were supposed to be my best friend. That means that you're supposed to know me like no one else. Shit, even Rich knows me. You know what he pointed it out last week? The fact that I don't like snakeskin. I like alligator skin. Cherie would've known that had she took the time out to learn me like I learned her."

"But you wear all the belts I've gotten you." She found herself pouting.

"Because you bought them. That's why I wear them. Thank you for the effort, but you failed. I'll tell you why. It's because I make everything about you. After all, you've gone through, I really thought that you deserved the best, so I gave it to you. What does Shane get? He gets you having to gravel in front of niggas."

"I saved your life!"

"Oh, eleven years after I saved yours. What? Is that all you got for me?"

"You can be a really mean asshole, you know that?"

"I wouldn't go hours without speaking to you or responding to your messages, but for some reason, it's cool for you to do that. However, I remember when you stormed into my damn house to jump down my throat over a misunderstanding. That's not what I need."

"Shane, we need to step away and meditate over this—"

"No. What we will do is step away altogether. I can't have hope in you, only for you to do the same shit. I refuse for my kid to grow up seeing her father so weak for a woman, but that woman keeps fuckin' up. She's going to think shit like that is okay, when it's not. By no means do I want her to hold on to a damn dream that won't come true. It's foolish and childish. It would've been a fairytale ending come true... but this is real life. Being at the Pavilion reminded me of that. And real life is the fact that I took you coming home for a funeral as you coming home to me. Well, I'm not that boy anymore, Cherie. I'm not going to always be here when you feel like coming back to me. I know I told you that I wasn't going anywhere, but fuck it. I don't have a choice. I can't live in my head anymore. I have a daughter to raise, and that ain't gonna happen if I'm salivating over something so farce or forced. It would've been nice, but it is what it is. Thank you for what you've done, but I can't accept any of it. Go live your life, man."

"Shane, just stop and listen to me!"

"Save your tears, Cherie. I'm done. You can do what you want."

"Listen, dammit!"

"Listen to what? How that nigga gave you head in the stockroom?"

Cherie's chest caved. How the hell had he known?

"Yeah, I had a setback and cross-referenced this nigga's number and name. Works up at the bar downtown, ten minutes from Royal Six's, might I add. He's an exotic dancer, too. His lil' patna told me about how much y'all see each other and how he knocked you down in the stockroom, then bragged about how sweet you tasted afterward. I believe his words were— *now that's what you call grown woman pussy.*"

Finally, tears spilled over. She didn't care to grab them.

"Let me ask you something. Did you know this motherfucker was legally married?"

"What?" she asked breathlessly.

"For the life of me, what I can't wrap my mind around is why you keep running from the one who knows you, will protect you, keep you stable, and who is not trying to hurt you. Obviously, you like those manipulative motherfuckers. I'll let you have them because I need to focus on my kid."

"You won't let me explain myself."

"I don't need you to." Hurriedly, he got into his SUV, slammed the door, and pulled off as if she wasn't standing there.

Cherie felt empty inside. She was hollow, and it was evident that the piece of her that she thought she gained was gone for good. They had a strong connection, but without one another they were merely weak.

A week later, Cherie straightened her black romper and ran her hand over her gleaming white diamonds that draped around her neck. She knew that she would need to sell even the jewelry that she wore, tonight. The driver of her rented SUV called to let her know that he was outside, waiting for her. Beautiful, classy and well put together, she got into her rental with her briefcases in hand. She was determined, over all else, to come home with a commission that could choke an elephant and to get her rocks off before doing so.

Unfortunately, thirty minutes into mingling, after setting up her pieces, she ran into Roxanna. She looked to have slimmed down. Her bandage dress was squeezing her body relentlessly. The ring on her finger wasn't the same as it was when Cherie left. Still, she approached her and tapped her on the shoulder. Roxanna turned around and surprised Cherie. Roxanna's eye makeup was smoky, yet she wore an insane amount of base and shimmer. Most likely to take away that fact that one of her eyes were swollen and was going down. Cherie remembered having to wear her eye makeup like that. With the new ring on her finger and the MAC on her face, it all pulled together. Roxanna was engaged to Terry, and it was evident. She had successfully traded places with Cherie, and from the looks of it, it wasn't so rewarding.

Roxanna's eyes bulged when they fell upon the new Cherie. Because of working, the stress of dealing with Shane and Davetta and the lack of eating, Cherie had dropped all of forty pounds within the last four months. Her dress hugged her curves so perfectly. It made Cherie look more womanly than she ever had, accompanied by her new short do. With the way that it stopped only two inches below her buttocks, it was a dress that Terry wouldn't approve of. Too bad that Roxanna thought that she was snagging something so seemingly perfect. In fact, when she heard of the jewelry party, she didn't contact Cherie to tell her that she had left Terry's friend for him. She wanted Cherie to see it for herself. To her dismay, her plan backfired. Cherie was more beautiful than ever, without an engagement ring or a man on her arm. Roxanna was heated inside.

"How are you, old friend?" Cherie greeted her, as she embraced the secretly angry woman. "I've missed you. I'm glad that you could come out."

Roxanna pulled back with egg metaphorically dripping from her face. Her expression was priceless with how she contorted it as if she was hiding her animated frown behind an equally animated smile. Roxanna was a mess.

"Mon Cherie, darling!" Roxanna cheered. "It's been how long since you've been gone?"

"Five months to be exact. How have you been?"

"Got myself in a little mix-up," she giggled, trying to flash the large blood diamond on her finger.

"Oh? And were you mixed up when you fucked Terry on the

island the day that I left?"

"Cherie, honey. The heart wants what it wants."

"It does," Damon said as he appeared at the side of Cherie. He pleasantly laid his hand on Cherie's hip after coiling his strong arm around her. That smile of champions beamed and almost blinded the hell of Roxanna. "Speaking of which...baby, shouldn't you start showing off your exquisite inventory?"

"Cherie?"

All heads turned to the voice that even Cherie didn't think that would be there. However, since Roxanna was present, it was only fitting that her owner wouldn't be too far behind. The poor, submissive tramp didn't know what she was getting into when she decided to accept Terry's proposal.

Terry walked up in his finest. The cufflinks on his gold and black velvet tuxedo jacket cost more than that of her flight from Richmond to Los Angeles. Same old Terry. He just had to be a showoff.

"Hello, Cherie," he greeted her, wrapping his arm around Roxanna's neck. The tension in Roxanna's body spoke volumes.

Cherie remembered feeling that tension when trying to pretend that everything was okay when it wasn't. She was smiling inside. "Hello, Terry," she spoke back.

"It's a pleasure for you to invite my fiancée and me to your shindig. I plan on draping her in the finest tonight." Terry stepped away from Roxanna, grabbed her hand gently, and kissed it for show.

"Good, because I have a lot for you to choose from."

"That you do, my love," Damon told her. "If you would excuse us, we'll be going now."

Cherie winked at Roxanna as she turned away.

Terry grabbed her by the waist and pulled her away from the crowd. He was seething inside. "Who the fuck was that?" he asked her through closed teeth. "That motherfucker ain't De'Shane."

"I don't know," she whined. "He didn't say his name. What's wrong with you?"

"Cherie's ass is supposed to be dead. That's what's wrong with me. And here she is selling fuckin' jewelry. Why didn't you tell me that this was her gathering?"

"I wanted her to see what she missed out on, Terry. I'm starting to think that you're not over her. And what do you mean that she's supposed to be dead?"

"Mind your goddamn business. That's what I mean."

"Terry—"

"Go and wait in the car, Roxy."

"But, baby—"

"I said go. You make it hard for me not to slap your ass in public, you know that?"

Fearful, Roxanna put her hideous four-inch heels in motion and bolted off to Terry's car. When she arrived, she sent Cherie a text that said that they needed to talk. Quickly, she erased it shoved it back into her purse so that her tears wouldn't fall onto her screen and give her phone any kind of water damage. Terry's statements didn't sit well with her. She was going to have to get to the bottom of it without his help. After all, Cherie was a very good friend to her, even though she climbed inside her fiancé's bed the first chance she got.

———————

"There ain't shit to discuss, Damon!" Cherie shouted inside her hotel suite. She snatched off her heels and tossed them over her bed. "You followed me here from Richmond. Why?"

"Baby, I had to speak to you," he pleaded. His attire was disheveled by now after all of the alcohol he drank and all the dances he shared with Cherie just to make the public think that they were happy. Angrily, he snatched off his bowtie and threw it onto the bed. "You've been running from me, and I need to know why."

"Could it be because you bragged about the sex we had? Huh? Or could it had been the fact that you were fucking legally married?"

Damon's neck bucked back. His lips slightly parted.

"You didn't think that I would find out? How about kids? You got those that you hadn't spoken of?"

"Now, hold on, Cherie. It ain't nothin' like that."

"Then explain your-damn-self."

"Look, I only got married to get the woman a green card. I didn't really know her all that well, and she was a fan."

"So, you just go around marrying fans all willy nilly?"

"Slow down now. I only forgot about it somehow."

"Forgot? Damon, that's bullshit. You don't forget marrying someone!"

"I was eighteen, and I was fuckin' drunk, Cherie! What about you? Huh? This Shane nigga. You're so caught up on him that you don't see a damn good man in front of you."

"I'm not caught up on Shane, so if I were you, I'd lay the hell off it."

"I'm laid. I'm going back to my room so I can head back to Richmond in the morning. I came out to support you and to show you that I still love you, but this is what I get. The both of you are made for each other. Y'all can have it."

"Fuck you too, Damon. You're the one who's legally bound to someone. What were you going to do? Wait until we filled out an application to be married and then spring it up on me then?"

"No, I was going to tell you before then, but you had a lot of drama on your end, so I didn't want to make it worse."

"Yeah, okay. That should've been discussed off-top."

"Whatever, woman. Just know that I love you and I'll see you when you get back to Richmond."

"Don't count on it."

Damon shook his head at her as he snatched up his tie from the bed so that he could leave.

Cherie folded her arms and plopped down on the foot of the bed. Her phone rang behind her. She rolled her eyes at it but reached for it just to see who it could've been. She knew that she didn't leave the gathering until ten, so it was one in the morning in Richmond. Who in the hell could've been calling her from home?

"Hello?" she answered.

"Rie, don't forget about my birthday breakfast in the morning," Quita said sleepily.

"Why the hell are you up, and you know I'm not going to forget about your birthday breakfast."

"Good, 'cause girl… Alyssa said she was coming and she had something to show us and tell us. I might need you to help me restrain Erykah's ass."

"Oh, Lord."

"That would be right. We need all the prayer and holy power we can get. Girl, I just got done with some micro braids that somebody wanted at the last minute, so you know I'm beat as fuck. What time are you landing?"

"I'm checking out in a little bit," Cherie sighed. "My flight leaves at two-thirty. I'll be landing by nine. I'll be at breakfast no later than nine-thirty."

"Okay, good. You know we ain't gonna start on time no way. We're colored folk."

"Shut up," Cherie giggled. "I'll see you in a little while, babes."

"Alright. Night."

"Night."

Cherie hung up and stood so that she could undo the zipper of her dress. Not once had she thought of seeing Shane at breakfast. She was trying so desperately to push him to the back of her mind and to leave him there. But she should've known that some things were harder said than done.

CHAPTER SEVEN

Faded To Sade

"Shane!" Rich called for him.

Shane squinted, trying to focus on each individual as he searched through the crowd inside Rich's new living room. Finally finding his old friend, he shimmied through the thick gathering with ease. He gave Rich their familiar handshake and shoulder-bumped one another.

"So, I need you to talk to somebody for me," Rich told him as he waddled from side to side. Shane could tell that his friend was more than tipsy. "See, she's cool people. She needs a distraction. I knew her back in school. She was a hermit, but she's cool. The nigga she had fucked over her. I fired him because I caught him trying to put his hands on her public. By fired... I mean I had him dropped in front of the barbershop."

"Rich, you know I can't—"

A young woman appeared at the side of Rich with a red plastic cup in her hand, a sad expression donning her caramel colored face. Shane noticed that her cheeks were rosy, and so was her perky nose.

She had been crying, he could tell.

"Richard, I'm just gonna go, okay?" she announced with high, upside-down V-shaped eyebrows. "I'll call you."

"Why? He's here."

"He, who?"

"Your distraction."

"My what?"

With a grin, he pointed to Shane. "Look, you and your dude been over for a minute, alright? You and my homie over here would click. If you don't, both of you can get a free lick in on me."

"What are we? Still in junior high? Please, Richard. You can't just push people into one another—"

"Shane," he finally introduced himself as he extended his hand to the damsel.

She squinted and focused on him. He wasn't the skinny boy with the afro. No. She barely recognized De'Shane. After junior high, she moved out of district, so she didn't get to see the transformation like most of their classmates had.

"April," she muttered. She then took his massive hand into her own.

"April Patterson, right? You were Deacon Patterson's daughter."

"Still am," she said on the heel of a giggle.

"You picked up some weight, didn't you? But not in a bad way. I barely recognized you."

She took her hand away from his and stood back to size him. "You damn sure picked up a lot of weight. I remember most girls didn't want to hug your cute little ass because they thought that you would've snapped in half had they tried."

"You got jokes, I see." Shane chuckled.

"Plenty of skinny jokes for the fat ones I feel like you're going to throw at me."

"Why would I joke about your weight?" Shane moved closer to her and leaned down to her ear to whisper, "More cushion for everything a grown man like myself has to offer." His hands slowly and gently latched onto her hips. "What's wrong with having a soft and fluffy grown woman between my palms? Hmm?"

Shane made April's spine tingle with the low rumble of his voice, his intoxicating cologne, his cool breath tickling her earlobe and neck, and the way he lightly squeezed her small love handles. Now she saw what other girls saw in Shane. It was his ability to make you melt when he wanted you to. But just like every girl knew, she did as well that he was Mon Cherie's property.

"Want to take a walk with me, April?" he asked once he pulled away.

Rich had long chased a skirt out of the back door of his new home and left the two standing there. April looked around as if she had actually come to the house party with someone, to make sure they didn't see her when she left, then took Shane up on his offer.

The two took all of an hour walking around the neighborhood, laughing and talking about how they knew each other in school but never really spoke to one another. After the stroll down Memory Lane, Shane dished that he had a daughter who was birthed by his deceased ex. April told him of her many miscarriages and of how her ex would act like he was too hard to show any emotion over them. They found out that they had service as a sin of theirs. That they both would wait hand and foot on their significant others. They learned that they loved too hard and didn't get what they put out into the universe back. Rich must've known what he was doing when he paired them up because April disclosed the fact that she had known that it was over between her ex long before it even came out of his mouth, but she clung to the fact that he was all she knew. Shane had to chuckle at that one and explain his situation with Cherie. The two exchanged numbers, and he walked her to her car so that she could finally leave. He tapped the hood and went to his Jaguar so that he could go and retrieve Miracle from Joyce's.

———————

When he arrived at the Big House, he noticed the twin Mercedes in front of the double doors which belonged to Quita and Erykah, and the Ford Escape that Alyssa was proud to be leasing. He narrowed his eyes, wondering what the trouble could be for them all to pile up at the house. Shane got out of the car and popped the collar of his black polo, then strolled into the house just to keep his cool. It didn't take long to find the women congregating at the dining room table in the dining room.

Quita was rubbing Erykah's back while Alyssa paced, and Mama J entered with a tray in her hands holding a kettle of hot water with teacups around it.

"Shane," she said breathlessly. "What are you doing back so early?"

"Came to get Miracle. What's this about?"

"Oh, honey. Just girl stuff."

"Rick is crying. I know that's girl stuff, but she rarely ever cries. What's wrong?"

Joyce pursed her lips and sat the tray down on the table. "Sweetheart, your sister is pregnant. She's just been concealing it."

"What?" he said with a hiss.

"The child's father wants nothing to do with either of them."

"Who is he?" His head whirled around to Erykah then, and his eyes blazed with anger.

"She's not going to tell you, De'Shane."

"Then what's his fuckin' address, birthday, height, weight... what? Throw me a fuckin' bone, Rick."

"No!" she cried. "Just leave it alone!"

"Why?" he shouted. "So you can be miserable! So he can just go Scott-free without taking care of his responsibilities? You for real?"

"I don't want nothing to do with him either! I just wanted my baby!"

"Speaking of babies," Joyce said soothingly. "Go on and have a little fun, Shane, okay? Miracle is down for the night. You don't have to work, you don't have anything else to do. Just go home or go for a drink or something."

"I can't drink on my meds, mama," he mumbled.

"Well, do something else with your life. She's fine, and I can handle Erykah. Go on, Shane."

"Fine. But the next time you have an issue, Erykah Marie… you need to come to big brother. I don't like to see you crying." Shane knocked on the table before he left, angry and all.

He thought about all the possible places he could go. The only place he could go to was the condo. Silence didn't sit well with him, though. He made a sandwich and walked around in his underwear and socks for a while. It was official. For the first time in a long while, Shane was bored. He decided to cruise through Richmond, thinking that something would spark his interest. When nothing hit him, he visited Jessica's grave in the dark of night to add a stone to her headstone and to wish her peace on her journey to the greater land. Afterward, he pulled his phone out to find two messages from April. She was wondering what he was up to if he was still awake, and if he would like a nightcap.

Shane received her address and went to her place. Before he got out of the car, he called Joyce to see if she was still awake.

"It's one in the morning," she told him with irritation in her raspy voice. "If I've been ignoring your texts, De'Shane, you know that everything is fine with Miracle. You better be on your way to the emergency room."

"No," he chuckled. "I just wanted you to know that I'm about to have a so-called nightcap with a lady friend."

"Shut your mouth!" Joyce sounded more alert as she sat up in bed.

"I am. Went by to say my goodbyes to Jessie, and now I'm in the parking lot of these nice looking apartments. I'm just… kind of afraid to go up because I don't know what to expect."

"Shane, baby, you're a grown man. Anything is possible tonight. You're baby-free and work-free. Get nasty for a change."

"I don't think I should be talkin' to you about things like this."

"Well that's too bad because I'm your mama, remember? May Chelle rest in peace. Still, you got to live life. You're about to be twenty-five. Live, boy. You done already dedicated your youth to other people. Go out and sew your oats, Shane."

He took a deep breath and shut off the engine to his Jaguar. "I guess you're right."

If you call me in the morning and tell me that you're taking this girl on vacation somewhere, I'm gonna slap you across the face."

"I'm sure I won't," he promised with a laugh.

"Good. Now, you leave Jessica and Cherie in the car before you go in there. I know you loved them, and I know you had a point to prove somehow. But, baby, it's all about what makes Shane happy now. This here is a start. Let something blossom that's pure and not by coincidence or association. Ya' hear?"

"I hear you, Mama."

"Lord, I can almost hear your daddy in my head. Him tellin' you to stop bein' so weak and to go on in there and handle your business before he would have to bust you in your chest."

"That's him you're hearing."

"Okay, baby," she giggled. "Go and enjoy your night. We'll see you for breakfast, right?"

"Breakfast?"

"Quita's birthday breakfast, Shane. It kicks off her week-long celebration. You know your daddy had y'all spoiled on celebrating all week. And Alyssa said she has something to get off her chest and something to show us all. So it's best that you enjoy your night, so to speak. I don't know what the hell is about to happen in the morning."

He sighed. "Alright, Ma. I'll see y'all in the morning."

"Night my love."

"Night."

Shane sucked up the last of his nervousness and got out of the car. It wasn't hard to find the apartment that he was looking for. He knocked quietly so that he wouldn't disturb her neighbors at this ungodly hour, then waited for her to open up for him.

The door came open. Shane had to lean back a little. April had let her black and wavy locks down. They curved around her slightly chubby face and accented the black, glossy Gucci frames of her reading glasses. She was dressed in what appeared to be an oversized baby blue dress shirt, with the cuffs unbuttoned, as well as the first three buttons on the chest. Shane could see her luscious bosom being held captive and squeezing together in her black laced bra. It almost made his mouth water.

"Thank you for coming," she greeted him below a giggle. "I didn't think you would. I thought that maybe it was too late."

"My mom has my daughter, and she won't let me take her until tomorrow."

April stepped aside to let him in, then took his leather jacket off for him.

Something caught Shane's ear and nose all in one instant. The distant sound singer Sade, cooing the lyrics of No Ordinary Love. He had to turn to look at her while she was closing the door. His nostrils tingled at the very faint smell of weed.

"Sorry," she shrugged with a smile. "I have a thing for nineties R and B, and I don't like to take pills for my nerves, so I... get lifted every now and again."

"Oh, no. You're fine. I love Sade...and... Jodeci...and... Boyz II Men."

"What about Dru Hill?"

"You talkin' to the right man."

April couldn't help but be captivated by Shane's smile. He was a true Casanova, and there was no use in fighting it. "Would you like a drink?"

"What you got?"

"Pretty much anything you can think of. You look like a cognac man. Am I right?"

"Actually, You are."

April swayed into the kitchen after laying Shane's jacket on the arm of her sofa. "I got Remy Martin Coupe Shanghai. Is that good enough?"

"You know...that'll work."

"Make yourself comfortable. It won't take long."

Shane took a seat on the couch, across from the sofa, and patiently waited for her to come back with his drink. As it was said, April returned with his drink and handed it to him. Then, she sat beside him and curled her feet underneath her bottom. Shane tried his best not to stare at her oiled, thick thigh between the split of her dress shirt as he sipped from his glass.

The smooth drink had to be held for a second so that he could savor the flavor. "Did you put Coke Zero in this?" he questioned with his eyes on the glass.

"I did," she answered with a light laugh. "You got good taste buds."

"I pay very close attention to detail. It's a gift and a curse."

"Really?" April was impressed. "Like, how close?"

"So close that I could tell you that you barely wanted to go out tonight with the way you wore your skippers with that army green spandex dress. And because you threw your hair in a ponytail was a dead giveaway that you only left the house at the last minute."

"Dang, you're good. That's exactly what happened."

"Told you, it's a gift and a curse. Oh, and you tied that denim jacket around your waist to try and hide your love handles because you didn't care enough to put on a waist cincher."

"Shane!" she squealed. "Stop reading me!"

"That's the curse part," he chuckled.

"Can I show you something?"

"Sure."

April took one last gulp of her drink. Then she sat it on the coffee table, took Shane by the hand, and led him inside of her second bedroom to show him what she had been working on.

The scent of wet paint stung Shane's nostrils before April could flick the light on. When she had, Shane's eyes adjusted and focused on a piece that was abstract but beautiful nonetheless. There was a woman on an eight-foot canvas, naked, stacking bricks in the painting. Her body looked tattered, bruised and scarred. In the background, there was a man with a blurry face. He stood with his arms over his wife beater. From underneath his armpit, he looked to be carrying a whip. Shane inched closer to the painting and eyed the detail. It's what April wanted him to do. There were so many small and meaningful details that made Shane want to touch them all.

"It's not finished," she mumbled from the door. "I usually don't show my work, but then again… I've always been made fun of for my visions. I was always told that I wouldn't be an artist. It was always called stupid shit and something that I was doing for attention."

"If only people were inside your head, then they would understand," he breathlessly muttered. Shane backed away a little and pulled his white V-neck shirt over his head to show April his tattoo. He had hoped that she would pay attention to it and tell him what it meant and tell him why she thought that he had it.

April reached out to his flesh and traced her cold fingertips over the outline of the bowing angel and his singed wings. Her lips itched to touch his muscular back. "He's so broken," she merely whispered. "He's ashamed, but he's trying."

"Right," Shane said quietly.

"He's beautiful, though. So much detail in your ink, Shane. Who did it?"

"A guy downtown by the name of Laughs."

"The white guy with the gray beard?"

Shane turned to her. Her eyes immediately fell on his impressive physique and the tribal tattoo along his collar. "Yeah, that's him," he told her.

"That… that's my boss," she admitted.

"Really?"

"Yeah, I just started there a few months ago."

"So, you tattoo?"

"Oh, Shane," she said with a sigh. "For some reason, there's a lot I feel like I should tell you."

"Apparently, I've got nothing but time. Let's do this."

Playfully, she rolled her eyes and lead him to her room. The first day of experiencing someone new was amazing. Shane was able to sit and laugh, talk, smoke and not come close to regretting it.

What felt like Shane only closing his eyes was actually him waking up. He found himself on the floor of April's bedroom. Fondly, his arms were wrapped around her, and she lay there so comfortable without a care in the world or a second thought to actually falling asleep in someone's arms.

Carefully, Shane slithered his arm from underneath her, found his shoes in the corner with his cellphone inside them. He checked the time, noticing that if he didn't get a move on, then he would be late to Quita's birthday breakfast.

"Leaving?" April asked in a raspy voice.

He looked down at her with a smile forming on his face. Still, he slid his feet inside his sneakers and found his shirt just beside his kicks. "My sister has her birthday breakfast to kick off a week-long celebration."

"Oh." April stood, stretching her limbs.

Shane's eyes were glued to her luscious body. When the hem of her dress shirt came up over her boy shorts, his eyes damn near fell out of his skull at the fatty that sat in the seat of her panties. If only he would've been savage with her the night before, then he would've known what she was carrying.

"Guess you got to go."

"I do," he responded quietly. Then, he approached her and gave her a gentle kiss on the cheek. "I enjoyed myself last night," he grumbled. "We have to do that again sometime soon."

Stuck On You 2

CHAPTER EIGHT

Been Missing Your Love

Mandy tried calling Rich for the umpteenth hundredth time in two days. Since he removed all of his belongings from her house, she was heartbroken. He left without so much as an explanation and a specific reason as to why he would leave her high and dry. After work, she threw off her shirt and carelessly tossed it over the back of the couch. Just as she flipped the light on to the master bedroom, there was a knock at the door. Hurriedly, she rushed to it in hopes that it was Rich possibly coming back to apologize or to tell her what the problem was.

Unfortunately, it was a tall, fair-skinned man with his salt and pepper curls greased to the back. There was something about his eyes that was so familiar to her. He reminded her of Cherie somehow.

"May I help you?" she asked nervously with narrowed eyes.

"Yes, actually. I was looking for Pat. Is she home? My name is Josiah."

"Umm... actually... my mom has passed. She's been gone for close to a year."

His once pleasant smile turned into a frown. He examined her closely as he thought of any other leads he could have. "Is... is Davetta near?"

"Give me a moment," Mandy said. She opened the door to let him in, then closed it while reaching into her back pocket for her cell phone. "May I ask why it is that you need to speak to my aunt?"

"I... uhh... your aunt? Right." Josiah appeared to be nervous. He rung his hands and couldn't stop rocking slightly from side to side. "Because... Pat was your mother."

"Are you alright?"

"Do you have a cousin that works at the boutique downtown? Uh... Royal Six's?"

"I don't believe so, but that's Erykah Cruz's boutique."

"The young girl who helped me one day... her name is Mon Cherie."

"Yes, that's my cousin. What business do you have with her?"

"Is she Davetta's daughter?"

"She is."

"I'm sorry... I didn't catch your name."

"Mandy."

"Okay, Mandy. I'm Josiah Devaughn. I used to... *see* Davetta about twenty-three, twenty-four years ago, and I need a few questions answered. Is there a way to get in touch with her?"

After tying two and two together, Mandy, with haste, called up Davetta and received the address to where she was staying. Then, she requested Cherie's number and gave the address to Josiah. Mandy didn't tell Davetta what it was for, but thankfully, Davetta gave it to her, thinking that she would've had a visitor finally. She didn't stop to think to ask Cherie if she was even back in Virginia to see if she could have any kind of company.

———————

Shane had arrived at the Big House, and every car was outside. He tried to pull himself together, by going up to his old room and finding something nice to throw on, then scurried into the hall bathroom to wash up and slip into his clothes. By the time he had gotten downstairs, and inside of the dining room, there were laughs and cackles to catch his ears.

"Hey, hey!" he called out, with his arms spread and a beaming smile on his face. That smile faded as everyone returned his greeting. His eyes landed on Cherie. *What the fuck is she doing here?* He located Joyce, who was holding Miracle and reached out for his daughter.

"Gone on," Joyce complained. "Shane, you have her every day. I don't."

"You might as well sit yo' ass down because I got next dibs," Quita said with a laugh.

"Just sit down and don't even look at her," Erykah teased. "We all got dibs. Ain't none of us working or in school, so she's gonna be passed around."

"Y'all on that other-other," Shane complained. He plopped down in the master's chair at the head of the table and laid his hands on his arms on the tabletop.

"What's wrong, baby?" Joyce asked him. "Night didn't go so well?"

"It was everything," he grumbled. "I need to see when's the next time we're going to be able to do something."

"What you did last night?" Quita asked with a frown.

"Smoked, drank, listen to Sade, fell asleep—"

"Mama, Shane out here hunchin'!"

"I didn't hunch nobody," he miserably said as he lifted his head. "She's cool people. That's it. Oh, and she's an artist."

"What kind of artist?" Erykah asked skeptically.

"She's a painter."

On cue, Shane's phone blared an unfamiliar song that made everybody look at him through narrowed eyes. He got up and dismissed himself so that he could answer it privately.

Joyce waited until Shane was away before she gave the girls a look. "Well, it looks like somebody is healing pretty nicely."

"Mama, don't," Quita said. "Next thing you know, he'll be buying her jewelry and trying to knock her up."

"Don't say that about your brother, Marquita."

"He acted like he didn't even see Cherie sitting here."

"Well, honey, Shane's head isn't over there for some reason. And as his sister— I'm sorry Cherie; you know I love you— your job is to move with the wave. There is no doubt that if in or out of a relationship with De'Shane that we're going to just pretend that Cherie doesn't exist. She's earned her place in the family. Unfortunately for us all, she's not your brother's option."

"And that's fine," Cherie added. "I'm just here to eat and enjoy my mimosas with my girls and the mother that I've earned within the last few months. Can we do that? Can we eat and get tipsy before the action later on? I've had one hell of a night, and I need something to take the edge off."

"What happened?" Quita asked her. She took it upon herself to pour the orange juice and champagne and to get it in rotation.

Cherie sat back in her seat, lowered her baseball cap over her tired eyes, then folded her arms over her bosom. "First of all, I run into the Roxanna chick that I told y'all about before. Then, here comes the puppet master who used to be engaged to me. Now he's engaged to her."

"What?" they all gasped in unison.

"Just trifling," Shane commented when he re-entered. He reclaimed his seat and laid his head back down on his arms.

Cherie rolled her eyes at him before she continued her story. "Anyway, the big kicker was the fact that before I held my showcase, in slips damn Damon to try to make me look good."

"Girl, stop!" Quita exclaimed.

"Wait, who's Damon?" Ashington asked. The others almost forgot that she was even present.

"You hush," Erykah warned her. "You're lucky that you're even sitting at this table. I should've put your ass upstairs to make you eat breakfast in front of the TV."

"Shane," she whined.

"I ain't in that," he grumbled.

"'Cause you're into something else," Cherie said under her breath. "Anyway, we go back to my hotel suite, and he has the nerve to give me all this bullshit about how much he just wanted to support me. Where the hell was his support when I actually needed it?"

"I'm home!" Alyssa sang from the foyer.

"We're in here, baby!" Joyce told her.

She swayed into the dining room with a glow to her, and everybody had scrunched brows. They were just waiting for her big surprise. To get down to the basics, she took off her leather jacket and turned around to show her family the beautiful collage that she had gotten. Luckily her stylish tank was backless. Everyone, excluding Shane, stood up and went to see the artwork that she spent a week getting inked into her flesh. It was a picture of Apollo in the middle with his hands in a praying position. Joyce peeked over one of his shoulders with her arm draped over the opposite. She wore a beaming smile on her face. All of his children surrounded them from pictures that she nabbed off of their Facebook pages. Below the portrait, on her lower back, was a dancing ribbon with cute cursive letters inside of it. It read, "Without family, we are nothing."

"Lyssa," Erykah said breathlessly. "This is beautiful."

"Girl, speak for yourself," Quita announced rudely. "I'm jealous as hell that I didn't think of this first."

"Alyssa, you know how your daddy felt about tattoos," Joyce stated with a smile. "But...this is a gorgeous and very generous portrait."

Ashington smacked her teeth. "Mama, she ain't ever gonna get married now."

"Didn't I tell you to hush?" Erykah reprimanded her.

"Y'all are trippin'," Shane mumbled, finally lifting his head. "Daddy almost shit a brick when he found out that I had gotten tatted. Shit, for a whole year, he didn't know about the one on my back. Seeing Michelle's name on my eyebrow, he was two-point-three seconds away from whacking me with his cane. He needs to be here to beat you for that."

"Boy… shut up."

"Nuh uh, Erykah," Quita intervened. "Daddy saw the rose on my thigh and went to strangle me. I was lucky that he restrained himself. He said that he didn't want his baby girl all marked up. Told me that I would never get a corporate job."

"Alright now, that's enough about your father," Joyce exclaimed. "Come on here so we can eat. Y'all know that if he were here, he would've been pissed because we didn't start breakfast on time."

"I'll help you, Mama J," Cherie offered.

Shane couldn't help but watch her as she left the dining room. Joyce handed Miracle over to Quita, and she secured the baby in her arms before slapping the back of her brother's head.

"You gon' miss her when she's gone," Quita commented.

Shane faced forward and stared at the wall. "She's already gone," he said softly.

Davetta opened the door to the condo and laid eyes on a man that could mold her over in the sack any day. Dressed in a pressed sky-blue dress shirt, starched gray slacks, and gray loafers, Josiah stepped through the door with his jaw clenching. He hadn't seen the hot mess of a woman since his wife threatened to kill them both for sneaking around.

"What're you doing here, Jo-Jo?" Davetta asked with attitude as she closed the door. To think that she ran through the house to tidy it up, and put on a good Maven shake-out wig was all for nothing. She didn't want to see him. Had Mandy told her who was coming, she would've given her the wrong address.

"Don't you call me that, Davie," he replied in a threatening tone as he sized her. "I left that crap back where I left my dang Fila's tennis shoes. You got something you need to be explaining to me, and I don't want no tears or excuses."

"What are you talking about, man?" Davetta folded her arms. She despised the fact that she had gotten out of her pajamas and slipped into a pair of jeans and tank top that hugged what little body she had. The blood between her and Josiah was rotten.

"I'm talking about Cherie, woman!" he roared, pointing to the door as if the young woman was standing there. "It ain't no secret that she looked like my daughter!"

"Excuse me?"

"You know what I'm talking about!"

"Oh, the daughter that you kept from me? While you were studying your law degree, Josiah? And that wife of yours that you never told me about before she damn near killed us both?"

"Answer me! Why didn't you tell me about Cherie?"

"Because she was none of your business!"

"You had my kid, Davetta!"

"And me living was more important than your fucking feelings! Your wife was going to kill us, so if I brought a baby to you and her, she would've been done with it all."

"You kept her away from me! You could've called me! I've had a daughter out there that I never knew!"

"And why the fuck is that important right now?"

"Because she's my kid, you insane woman?"

"You need to get two things straight." Davetta took two long steps to close the space between her and Josiah. With seriousness in her face, she stuck her chest out to explain, "You better not ever forget who the fuck put you through law school during your final year. That little uppity bitch you wifed knew nothing about it and probably wasn't woman enough to do it like I did. Lastly, you broke my heart, Jo-Jo. You chose her over me, and then you wrote me a bullshit letter about how your daughter meant the world to you and how you wanted her to have both her parents. So I gave you what you wanted, and at the same time, I decided to break your goddamn heart right back. You never saw or knew Cherie, and you never will. You weren't going to put her on the back burner, ever. You need to get the fuck out of *my* daughter's house."

"Davie, you don't understand—"

"I said get out!"

"Jessica was murdered, Davetta!" he shouted. "I already lost one daughter. I can't fathom losing another. I don't care how bad you fucking hate me. I deserve the right to see my kid."

"She's a grown woman, Jo-Jo, and you don't deserve to see shit. Now, I'm sorry about Jessica, or whatever her name is—"

"What about Jessica?" Cherie asked. She slowly closed the door to her condo with both their eyes on her. "What *about* Jessica?" she repeated herself, this time with her eyes on Josiah. "What's going on? How do you know where I live, and why are you two yelling at each other?"

"Cherie, we need to talk," Josiah began.

Davetta cut him off. "This here is your daddy," she said rudely. "He's the motherfucker that could've saved us both a lot of pain and suffering. He's the motherfucker that took all my damn sense and confidence. Yeah, that's him. Go on and say hi."

Cherie didn't know whether to be upset at the fact that Davetta was rude in introducing her to her father in that manner or to fall out onto the floor when finding out who he was.

"I'm sorry that we have to meet like this—"

"Give me your number and get out of my house," she blurted.

"Excuse me?"

"I said… give me your number and leave. I have a lot of things that I need to think about."

"Cherie—"

"It's *Mon* Cherie, and no wonder you were staring at me like that in the store. No wonder you wanted to know what my name was."

"You looked so much like my Jessie that I had to stop and ask you." Josiah found a notepad on the bar, near the cordless phone that Cherie rarely ever used, and scribbled his information on it. Then, he handed it to her and took his leave.

As soon as the door closed, Cherie dropped the pad and whacked Davetta across the face.

Hopeless, with the force of her daughter's hand, Davetta fell to the hardwood floor and skidded a few feet. She held her cheek and looked up Cherie with shock in her eyes and blood dripping from her mouth.

"I've been wanting to do that for years," Cherie said low and angrily. "You pick yourself up off that floor and get to explaining this to me, Davetta."

CHAPTER NINE

Light Another Blunt Up

April sat in the first row as the auction persisted. She was shivering, knowing that her piece was up next. The auctioneer decided to have an open bidding. She was so nervous that she couldn't grab her purse from the floor to text Shane, just to see if he was in the building.

"Any takers?" The White man grinned as he searched the crowd for paddles of anyone who could start the bidding.

Without hearing anyone at all speak, April was becoming angry. Everything that her ex had said about her art being a joke and that no one would take it seriously was coming to reality.

"Twenty-five!" a man called out amusingly.

"Well, alright. That's twenty-five. Can I get thirty? Anyone? Going once, going twice—"

"Thirty!" Another man shouted.

April was fuming. How could they pay so little for what she worked so hard for? Something that looked like splashed paint on a canvas sold for a hundred times as much, yet hers is made a mockery of.

"Going once. Going twice—"

"Five thousand dollars."

April had to stand and damn near snap her neck to see who could've bid that much.

Down the aisle came a taut young man in a pair of black slacks, black vest, a gold dress shirt that was rolled up at the elbows, and a metallic gold tie. In his massive hands, he counted out his funds and had them correct by the time he reached the podium. He placed the stack on the fine cherry wood, then brought his paddle out from under his arm.

"My name and address are on that paddle," Shane told him with a grin. "I'll be expecting my painting in the morning."

Shane turned to April to see the shocked expression on her face. Her hand was cupped over her mouth and tears were flowing down her cheeks.

"You... you paid... for my art."

"Of course I did. I told you that I was a collector. I need that on my wall when I move."

"Shane... can we go home now? My social anxiety is really kicking in."

Happily, Shane took her by the hand and escorted her out of the building.

"How did you know that I was here?" she quizzed.

"You told me that your portrait was going to be auctioned off at a benefit for Lupus," he explained. "Even though you didn't tell me where I looked it up online. I hope you didn't think I was going to let a piece like that slip up under my nose."

April couldn't stifle her smile.

"How did you get here?"

"Borrowed my sister's car."

"Well, take it back to her. I'll follow you. You shoot pool?"

"Do I?"

"Good," he chuckled.

Finally, they reached the street. April fished her ticket out of her clutch and handed it to the valet. Shane pecked her cheek before taking his leave. He followed her as he mentioned, and waited for her to go inside her sister's house and to come and sit in the passenger seat of his Jaguar. Only, when she returned, she wasn't wearing the smile that showcased the dimples that he was growing accustomed to.

"What's the matter?" he asked her.

"Nothing," she lied.

"Come on, April. You know I pay attention. Tell me what happened."

She waited for Shane to pull away from the curb just so that he wouldn't go in there and lay hands on her brother-in-law. "I just get so tired of being the butt of every joke," she expressed. "He always has something to say, and she just sits there like it's okay."

"He, who?"

"My brother-in-law. Tucker. And do you think my sister will stick up for me?"

"What did he say?"

"Oh, I'm not telling you."

"And why not?"

"Shane... I've dealt with a crazy man before, alright? You give off the same vibe. I mean, I don't mean to compare you two, but I will tell you that you have the same essence as he does."

"Okay. If I promise not to put my hands on Dude, would you tell me what he said?"

"Fine." April huffed and took out the butterfly clip in her hair. She fluffed her curly locks and looked over at him with a tilted head. "He said that he should've known that I was at the house because everything was starting to gravitate toward me. That the digital signal in the house has depleted. Then he looked at my sister and asked her why she keeps letting this planet of me in the house."

"Oh, word? We're telling fat jokes now?"

"Shane, don't worry about it, okay?"

"You know, the best revenge is success."

"I know that. But there was no need in saying it because I wasn't successful at anything."

"Yes, you are. Your painting just got sold for five stacks."

"And that's it."

"Why do you do that, April?" he asked honestly. "Why do you do this to yourself? You down the hell out of yourself because of other people."

She sucked in a breath to say something, but the great and powerful Shane had to stop her.

"Don't sit there and tell me that you don't, because I can see it in your face and heard it in your voice when you tried to protect old boy back there. You take the blame for everybody being dumbasses. I'm going to need you to stop doing that."

"But—"

"Stop." Shane looked over at her as a smirk stretched across his lips. "...or else you'll get a spanking."

Playfully, April swatted at his arm, then took her attention back to the road.

"Let's go and enjoy our night, alright? That's without anyone and their bullshit."

On cue, his cell phone lit up in the holster on the dashboard. He could see that it was an employee, yet he had no idea what he could've wanted. Shane snatched the phone, pressed it to his ear, then pushed his head into the headrest. "Yeah?"

"Shane, we got a little issue," the man said.

"What is it?"

"We, somehow, went over quota. Rich ain't answering his line, so we need you to come and scoop your dough. Go on and make payouts, if you will. We double-checked everything, but we still over quota."

"I'm on my way." Shane hung up and looked over at April for a split second. "We have to make a stop... obviously."

"Shane, are you a—"

"Yes, I'm a *boss*." He grinned and looked back at her. "Any more questions?"

She blushed and looked away from him so that he wouldn't see it.

Moments later, Shane had parked, gotten out and come back to the Jag with a few duffle bags, yet he wasn't holding any. He popped the trunk and waited for the men he knew to load them up before he could take off. Without a stray strand or thread of his clothing out of place, he slid back inside of his driver's seat and pecked her on the cheek.

"Did you miss me?" he asked her innocently.

"Why do you do that?" she giggled.

"Do what?"

"Kiss my cheek?"

"Because I love your dimples." He threw her a wink and pulled away from the curb.

––––––––––

By the end of the night, Shane and April were two good looking people who ended up at Dave and Buster's, having a blast. Shane took April home, and they had yet to stop laughing and talking about the past. They stumbled into the apartment, a little tipsy, and still had yet to check their phones. Their devices were not important. Their happiness, however, was.

April made drinks while Shane undid his necktie and slipped out of his vest. When she made it inside of her bedroom, she sat the glasses down on the nightstand and helped Shane out of his dress shirt. The tattoo that peeked from over the curve of his muscle shirt begged to be licked and kissed. She only ran her tongue gently across her lips while suppressing the longing of having this man all to herself for the night.

Shane eased his hands around April's waist and smoothed up her soft back until he found the zipper between her sequin flaps with his fingertips. Slowly, with his eyes prying into hers, he unzipped it. Carefully, he peeled it off of her. Ever so slowly, he unveiled her curvy body. He noticed the tension in her stature as he stared, at how she lightly shivered. April was insecure.

"You're going to fuck around and find me happy with someone else, and it won't be my fault," she remembered saying to her ex. Her words were coming to fruition. It scared her.

"And Shane... try not to fall in love too early." He could hear Joyce in his head clearly as he eyed April's body closely.

One kiss to her neck he painstakingly delivered, sending shivers up her spine. Finally, she gave in, wrapping her arms around his neck.

———

Cherie ran her fingers over the silky fabric of her headscarf before stepping out of the car. She was hesitant about approaching Mandy after so long, but if anybody could understand where she was coming from and help her figure herself out without judgment, it would've been her cousin. She could've easily gone to Erykah or Quita since they were all their father's children but hadn't known officially until recently, but this task was a little too real for them all, so to speak.

Cherie knocked on her aunt's front door in hopes that Mandy would answer. After hearing Davetta tell her that Mandy and Rich were no longer together, they were technically in the same boat. Her love's ex was her sister, and that in itself was a heavy load to carry.

Looking a mess in her tight-fitting tank top and her loose pajama bottoms, Mandy brought the door open. Cherie cocked her brow at her cousin's disheveled hair.

"It's that bad, huh?" Cherie asked her.

"You have no idea. Get in here."

Mandy knocked back three mimosas while explaining to her cousin how Rich up and left while she was away from the house. Since then, he had yet to return a call. His own mother didn't bother to pick up for Mandy.

Cherie gulped down the single glass that she had been babysitting at the breakfast nook. Then, she slammed it down on the table when it was empty. Her eyes were hard on Mandy. "What the hell is wrong with everybody?" she questioned. "First, Shane has a whole new damn attitude, then he shows up at Quita's birthday breakfast after he's been out all night, and now I find out that his ex, Jessica, may she rest in peace, is my sister."

"The fuck?"

"Her old man was in my condo. He was screaming at Davetta about something, and she was screaming right back. I'm betting money on the fact that he didn't know anything about me. Shit, I'm not even going to ask why that was. I'm just going to say that Davetta has done more shit than a little bit to—" Cherie's ringing phone distracted her. It was Roxanna's ringtone, yet there was no call. Only a text. She squinted at it, then replied.

"What is it?" Mandy was curious. Something had washed over

her cousin like disgust and anger.

"This bitch said she needs to talk to me. She has nothing to say to me after she done up and got engaged to my leftovers."

"Shut the fuck up!" Mandy sang. "Wasn't she your ace, though?"

"*Was.* Keyword."

"Either way… Shane, Rich, or what's his face… they ain't ever gonna find women like us. Fuck 'em all."

"You got that shit right."

"*He said that you should've been dead, Cherie,*" the text read. "*That doesn't strike you as odd? I knew you were alive, and so did our little clique. What the hell? He was very angry to see you. He assumed that you would've been with Shane. He's been drinking heavily and making phone calls since you left.*"

"*He's your problem now, not mine. I would appreciate it if you stopped contacting me,*" Cherie replied. Then, she blocked Roxanna's number and placed her phone face-down on the table.

"These hoes are a trip, cousin," Mandy said with a giggle. "Are you up for a little retail therapy?"

"Can you afford it?" she asked skeptically.

"Shane paid off the house. I'm good."

"And when the hell did he make that financial decision?"

Mandy shrugged. "You were in California when the bank was breathing down my neck about it, so he put the money up."

"Then… let's go."

That was the only thing to bring a genuine smile to her face. She hadn't even bothered to ask her cousin if she could afford their little trip. She only assumed that Cherie was balling since she was selling jewelry now. Certain things could bandage a bleeding heart, and shopping was most definitely one of them.

Shane walked circles around the tables dressed with his work inside the Cruz warehouse. In the distance, he could hear the money counters chattering away, adding up his funds. He eyed the work, but only with a certain swing in his steps. It was almost as if he was dancing around the table as opposed to walking.

"Fuck got into you?" Rich asked from the hood of his car, only yards away from his friend.

"Nothin," Shane chuckled.

"Lyin' ass! What's up, bruh?"

"Ain't shit," he assured Rich.

"Nigga… I know you. It ain't the meds that got you like this. You dug into April Patterson, didn't you?"

"Maybe."

"Maybe my tip, dude! You smashed April? The deacon's daughter?"

While Rich was being dramatic, Shane hopped up on the hood of the BMW that Rich bought weeks prior with a grin on his face. He took his time to run the crease on each leg of his heavily starched jeans through his fingertips before he answered. "I ain't gon' lie… the deacon's daughter might as well be the goddess of freak nasty."

"Oh! Nigga! You did!"

"It's just somethin' about her, Rich. She's so—" Before he could finish, the chorus of Emeli Sande's song "Somebody" blared from his back pocket. He placed his pointer finger up to his lips as a signal that he needed Rich to stay quiet for a second.

"Oh, okay. And now you gon' shush me so you can talk to lil' Roli Poli Olie over there. Alright. I gotchu, bruh."

"Nigga, you hooked us up."

"Well, forgive me. All this shit is my fault. I can't even talk to my nigga now, because I got him a new chick, and he want to stay caked up while we're supposed to be workin'! My bad, folk!"

"What?" April asked.

Shane swiftly turned away from Rich, not knowing that she could hear Rich after Shane had answered. "My fault, boo," he softly explained. "That's just Rich. You know he's an asshole. No need in me telling you that. So, what're you up to?"

"Nothing." She sighed. "I was just invited to my niece's birthday party."

"Oh?"

"Yeah. I was wondering if..."

"If, what?"

"If you weren't too busy later... maybe... you would like to go with me."

"Of course," he chuckled. "I'm all up for it."

"Great. So, I'll see you at seven?"

"You got it, gorgeous."

"Don't make me blush. I'll see you later."

"Bye, boo."

"Bye," she sang.

"So, what's that about?" Rich asked annoyingly. "You finna marry her now?"

"Tell me somethin'." Shane adjusted himself on the hood of his best friend's car while staring at the workers who were bagging up his money in front of him. "Have you ever noticed something strange about April?"

"What you mean? Other than her being a hermit?"

"The other day, she told me that her brother-in-law said some cruel shit to her—"

"That dude, T-Mac? Tucker from Bonnieville?"

"I guess."

"Yeah, he rips on her all the time. You know him. He used to play basketball for the school. Remember? He was in the eighth grade when we were in the seventh. He dropped out of school junior year to trap. He worked for your old man. Well, now he works for you. But he's a dick, bro. Don't pay him no mind."

Shane rubbed his chin while thinking. Tucker really hurt her feelings the other night. Shane had a plan for that. He was going to put a stop to it.

CHAPTER TEN

Intense Now

Cherie placed her shopping bags on her bed so that she could relax for the rest of the day. She didn't approve of how Erykah wasn't working lately. They were taking online orders for now. When Erykah redid the website, she made sure to place three stars next to the sentence that she typed in bold. It read that each customer should expect for their product to return to them between six to eight weeks. Each piece that was in stock should be received no more than three weeks after the order was placed. Even though it cut out her commission, for the time being, she was fortunate enough to make commission off of what she sold when she was in California. Her condo was paid up for six months, so that wasn't an issue. Besides, she had money in savings that would keep her afloat for the rest of the year. Hopefully, Erykah would come out of whatever stupor she was in before Cherie was forced to find another job.

"Can we talk?" Davetta asked her from the doorway of her room.

"No," she chimed. "You can go to your room or fly to Mars for all I give a fuck, Davetta. You put me through too much shit for me to even look you in your face, but I tried my best to make peace with you. Now all of a sudden I have a whole damn daddy. Do I need to remind you that my supposed sister is my ex's ex?"

"I'm sorry."

"Keep your apology. You've fucked up too much of my life for me to even begin to think about forgiveness."

"Are you... are you gonna call him? Josiah, I mean."

"Maybe...and if I am, that has nothing to do with you."

"Mon Cherie, I'm sorry!"

"Please get out of my face."

With a frown, Davetta turned away to leave.

Cherie had to ask her an important question before she left. "Did you hear your man say anything about his son wanting me dead?"

"What?" Davetta's brows furrowed. "What type of shit is that to ask me?"

"Roxanna told me that Terry mentioned the fact that I was supposed to be dead."

"I ain't ever heard no shit like that."

Cherie looked down at the floor. Maybe he told Roxanna that because he may have thought that the mob was going to come after her. That's what she thought, and that's where she left it. For now.

The shopping almost helped, but it wouldn't help the gnawing feeling that she had in her mind of wanting to call Shane and ask him why he hadn't been as affected as she was over their separation. She knew that the new chick he was spending so much time with was distracting him, but she wanted to know why. Why was it so easy for him to be okay with the arrangement? Most of all, she wanted to tell him about Jessica being her sister. Until she had gotten enough courage to do so, she phoned Alyssa and Quita to see if they felt like clubbing tonight.

"Shane!" April squealed. She was trying her best to hold on to the handle of the Big Bass Pro game. It had broken, but April wanted her tickets.

Reluctantly, Shane came over and helped her to hold down the lever so that she could get as many tickets as she could.

Soon after, most of the little girls at April's niece's party was running Shane left and right so that he could help them out too. They especially wore him out on the basketball and the skeeball game. Even if he wanted to say no, he wasn't going to be able to. They put the sweetest eyes on him and made him assist them anyhow. He wondered if Miracle would grow to be that way. Bat her lashes or present her gorgeous eyes all a twinkle, just to get her way.

He was able to sit for a while as April's niece opened her gifts. He was okay, though he was tired, all until he excused himself to go to the restroom to wash his hands before he ate. When he emerged from the restroom, he almost bumped into Nicola, April's sister. He tried to pass her until he thought of the eyes that she was giving him from across the room. She, along with a few other women who were invited, kept staring and whispering while he playfully fed April the custom ordered pizza that he had a hankering for. She tooted her nose up at his veggie supreme pizza with white cheddar cheese. Because of it, he had to force-feed her his own little concoction. But from afar, he could see the jealousy written all over Nicola's face that her sister had the better looking, richer, more involved man.

Shane backed away from Nicola with his brows pressed together. Then, he looked down at the arm of his Givenchy Rottweiler graphic sweatshirt that sprouted out from beyond his sleeveless denim jacket as if she hurt him when she only gently touched his bicep.

"Come on now," she cooed. "I saw the way you were looking at me, Shane."

"Lady, one, I was only lookin' at you because you were starin' at your sister and me. Two, this sweater costs more than your damn rent, so don't dare touch me. Three, I'm your sister's man, you classless ass broad. Four, we're at your daughter's party. At least try to push up on a nigga during an adult party or some shit. Lastly— weak ass woman— if I ever hear about your dude makin' inappropriate comments about April again… it's lights out for both of you. Well… more so for him. I'll just have somebody fuck you up a lil' bit to teach you a thing or two. Now, back the fuck up off me before I tell your sister and your man about how much of a hot twat you got."

"You wouldn't. It's not like either of them would believe you."

Shane dropped his head and chuckled. Then, he adjusted his designer silver framed specs on his face and tipped the brim of his fitted cap at her. "I'm your man's boss," he told her. "He'll listen to whatever I got to tell him. April? She's head over heels for me, so don't count on her fallin' for some poppycock alligator tears if you decide to let some out." Lastly, Shane threw two fingers at her during his exit out of the slim hall to get back to April.

Nobody knew about Shane deciding not to take his meds anymore. He only put on a good front for the others, and it worked. He didn't need them anyway. His life was great. Shane was even planning on letting April meet Miracle after he picked her up from Josiah's in the morning.

Once he returned to the table where April was mindlessly going through her phone before he left, he found that she wasn't there. He searched through the millions of gaming machines for a while and settled on the fact that she might've been outside.

"You weren't invited," she stressed, as soon as Shane opened the front door.

"I was invited by T-Mac, and you know that. He told me that your new nigga was here, and I don't give a fuck about him. I'm here to see my niece," Sisco, her ex, expressed.

April folded her arms and looked off to the side of her. If she knew Shane like she was supposed to by now, then she should've kept her eyes forward.

"Look, don't act like you don't miss me."

"I don't," she fired off. "Don't flatter yourself."

"Me? Don't flatter *myself*?" He took another step to tower over her. His six-foot even height engulfed hers. His dark skin glistened with anger. She wasn't the same woman who took anything he said or feared him the way that he had hoped. "Girl, you better remember who the fuck you're talkin' to. Whoever this nigga is only wants you because he has a fat girl fetish. Ain't nobody ever gonna want you. Why you think you wasn't invited to this motherfucker when everybody else was? Nicola and Tucker don't give a fuck about you, girl. Nobody does. Even the so-called nigga that Tucker told me you was hugged up w—" All of his words stopped when he felt cold steel pressed at the back of his neck.

Curious as to why he shut up the way he had, she looked over at him through lowered lids. She gasped at seeing the menacing man behind the one who used to drop a heavy fist onto her soul. Her heart rate shot up through the roof at realizing that Shane had his gun held on the back of her ex's neck.

Sisco's hands slowly rose as a sign of defeat. You could literally see the wannabe thug trembling out of fear. Where'd all his vigor and harassment go?

"Get your midnight ass in your car before I light you the fuck up," Shane quietly warned him through gritting teeth. "It's about to be dawn for you, Midnight. You sure you wanna go this route?"

"Baby," April quietly called him. Her face didn't show her fear. Her body spoke otherwise as well. "Please put the gun—"

"Oh, so this is your pussy ass nigga?" Sisco taunted her. "Shit, I thought I was gettin' robbed." With a cocky demeanor, he turned around to shout some more insults, all until he realized who was holding a gun at his side now. Sisco's eyes grew the size of golf balls when he identified his very own boss there. There wasn't one man in Virginian territory who didn't know not to fuck with Shane The God. He had more than screws loose. It was one thing messing over Shane's father's money, but he was messing with The God's woman. One who used to be Sisco's own. "Boss man?" he asked nervously. "You... this you?" He then pointed over his shoulder with his thumb toward April. "This wifey, right here? Man, I didn't know."

April huffed as she moved past her punk ass of an ex, and massaged the chest of Shane's sweater. "Can we not?" she asked innocently. "We were having such a good time. I still have tickets in my purse that I want to turn in. Remember, you promised my niece that you would help her get more tickets to get that beach ball. You can't do that if you're duckin' the laws. Can we go back inside? Please?"

"Yeah, baby," Shane smirked. "You go on. I just need to get a word in. If you want to, you can take my piece and put it in your purse."

Having an uneasy feeling about Shane going up against Sisco, she happily took his gun away and placed it inside of her purse. She gave him one last look before scurrying away with a heavy heart. Everything that Sisco said was true about her family, and she knew so. They waited this late to invite her to her own niece's birthday. They must've booked the spot almost a month in advance, yet they waited. She didn't understand why they did her so wrong, but she wasn't going to try and figure it out either. With Shane, their hurtful blows were like tickling her with a feather.

"Look, whatever y'all got goin'—"

Sisco couldn't finish his statement with how quick, and hard Shane socked him in the mouth when April closed the last door to the entrance. He hit the ground, holding his mouth.

"See, it's niggas like you that make it hard for men like me," Shane angrily explained. "You get a good one, and you decide to rip her to shreds instead of taking care of her. But don't you worry her no more. I'm takin' damn good care of her, and ain't you fired?"

"Rich—"

"Got your pussy ass jumped. Stay beneath her, nigga. You ain't worth the time."

Sisco watched as Shane left with what little bit of manhood that he had left.

"Baby, we need to go." Shane reached April, helping her out of her booth.

"What happened?" she panicked, trying to keep up with his quick strides to the ticket counter.

"I'm just no longer comfortable here, and I highly believe that you're not wanted here. If it wasn't for your niece, we would be headed toward the door."

He pulled his wallet out, handing the cashier a $50 bill. "Give me that beach ball up there, and take it to the birthday girl at the back, will you?"

"Shane… what's going on?"

Gently, he pulled her by the hand, escorting her to the car. Lucky for her that Sisco wasn't on the ground at the time that they exited. She would've seen the damage Shane had done anyway after she left.

"Shane, now you're scaring me," she managed as he stuffed her into the Jaguar to leave.

"I don't want to be here."

"That's obvious, but what happened?"

Shane slammed the door and started the car. He had to get himself together before he seriously lost all control. "April, baby… I don't like how you're being treated. Forgive me for having feelings for you. Matter of fact, don't. These people look down their noses at you, for crying out loud. For what, I don't know. I'm not even going to try and figure it out. If we don't get out of here, I might end up cussin' everybody the fuck out, and you're really going to look at me differently."

Hanging on to the last of his solitude, Shane reached over April's lap to open his glove compartment. Quickly, he grabbed his bottle of Seroquel, unscrewed the cap and popped two pills into his mouth so that he could chew them.

"Shane..." April's voice quivered as she watched in awe. "What... are those? Why are you taking them?"

"April, let me scare you off now." After shoving the pills back into the compartment, he stared over into her shocked, prying eyes. "I have a serious disconnect from reality, alright? That, in the glove box, is Seroquel. Do you know what that is?"

"It's... an anti-psychotic medication."

"Exactly. That means that I'm crazy. Weeks before I met you, I had come home from a mental institution. If you want to walk away from me, you may do so now. If not, here are some of the things you may experience. One, I may pull the trigger the next time you're threatened by another man. Two, I may end up firing that brother-in-law of yours or stomping him out. Three, I tend to have jealous rages that I'm learning to control, so we'll put a star next to that one because it may or may not occur."

"Shane—"

"Let me finish."

"Your nose."

"What?"

"You're bleeding!"

Shane hurriedly pulled the visor on his side down so that he could look into the mirror. Sure enough, he was bleeding. Crimson touched his top lip, warm and thick.

April rummaged through the compartment to grab a few tissues and hand them to him. Shane stuffed a corner of it up his nostril and mashed the gas to get April home so that he could go to his own. He hadn't known where his sudden headache had come from before he could shut off his car, yet he chose to ride the wave of it and thought that he could kill it off with Ibuprofen. With nothing helping, he chose to make phone calls around two in the morning to let his family know that he was going to have to go to the emergency room. He had developed dizzy spells, even when laying in bed, and he had to jump up to puke more times that he could count. When he looked at himself in the mirror, he didn't see Shane. His skin was a shade paler; there were dark rings around his eyes. The trip to the hospital was needed. Something went wrong. Wrong indeed.

CHAPTER ELEVEN

New Additions & Late Arrivals

Cherie stepped off the elevator before Erykah could. She, along with the Cruz girls, minus Ashington, marched down the corridor in their six-inch pumps and their club attire with their hearts racing. Shane wasn't one for hospitals. He despised them. Something had to be entirely wrong for him to volunteer to come to one. They could hear him screaming from the room where they were told that he was being held. Cherie sped up the pace in her heels, almost jogging, to get to him before someone would wind up hurt.

Before she reached the door, a short and stocky Asian man skidded over the threshold as he adjusted the specs on his face.

"Doctor?" Cherie assumed. "Are you a doctor?"

"Yes," he assured her. "I'm Dr. Wong. I oversaw Shane during his stay at the Pavilion."

"What's wrong with my brother?" Quita asked him.

From where Shane was laying in his bed, squirming to get over the burning sensation of what his primary care provider placed inside his IV, he could hear them talking. He was experiencing a floating feeling when he heard Dr. Wong tell his sister that he was experiencing a stronger disconnect from reality.

"*Disconnect*?" He heard Cherie's voice.

"Rie," he softly and pathetically called her. He tried to add volume to his voice, but there was nothing. "Rie," he merely whispered.

Over him appeared to be the sweetest face he'd ever seen after calling out for her. Cherie could feel Shane's fear. She latched on to his hand as he tried his best to sit up. She laid a gentle hand on his chest to comfort him and to make him lie back down. Tears welled in her eyes. The pit of her stomach knotted. She felt a little guilty that she didn't catch on to his disconnect a while ago. Maybe she could've helped him. Maybe there was a way for her to catch him before he slipped. She felt that it was her fault for letting him live inside of his head for so long.

"Shane," she cooed no higher than a whisper. "Baby, listen to me, okay? You have to lay back and let your meds work. You have to stop trying to fight it. I'm here."

"But Rie—"

"Lie down. I'm here."

"Am I going to die?"

The question struck her. She didn't know what to say to him. A few months ago, he was so ready to leave. It left her wondering what had changed.

"Am I crazy?"

Even that question slapped her across the face. "Sleep, Shane," she demanded quietly.

"Don't go." On cue, his eyes rolled into the back of his skull. Whatever was in his IV had finally put him out.

———

Cherie paced in the waiting room. Erykah rocked in her chair with her the thumbnail of her left hand caged between her teeth. She was a worried wreck. Quita stepped off the elevator from going to get coffee. Ashington was right beside her. Her duty was to get everyone a change of clothes and to get Erykah's car to the hospital safely.

One by one, they took turns to change clothes while the others waited in case a doctor had come to let them know of Shane's condition. Once they were all clad in either pajama bottoms, undershirts, basketball shorts, sweats, leggings or tank tops, they all sat and waited some more.

The elevator dinged, but the pair to step off wasn't one that anybody expected to see. Rich went to Alyssa, pulled her out of her seat and wrapped his arms around her waist tightly. The others had contorted faces, trying to figure out what the hell was going on between the two.

Quita closely surveyed the short and fluffy woman that Rich brought with him. She didn't look like Rich's sister, so Quita folded her arms and sat on the arm of Ashington's seat. "And who might you be?" she asked aloud.

"Oh, I'm… I'm April," she introduced herself. "I'm, uh… a friend of Shane's."

"His *girl*," Rich said for her as he turned to the confused faces in the waiting room.

Cherie stood out of her seat with a cocked brow. Ashington, in turn, rushed over to her to place a gentle hand on her shoulder. Cherie slapped it down. "His girl, huh?"

"Don't start no shit."

"Rich, just keep your damn mouth shut right now. You're four hours fucking late coming to see about him anyway."

"You're still eleven damn years behind, but ain't nobody jumpin' down your throat."

"That ain't even called for!" Erykah bellowed. "Now you can talk to Rie like a fuckin' adult, or you can get the fuck out. But since we want to poke at wounds, why the fuck are you here with my sister and not checkin' up on Mandy? You know... the chick you pussied out on?"

"Mind your own. It ain't my fault that Alyssa wanted to keep us a secret. I was being respectful to what she wanted."

"You know what..." Quita stood with her hands in the air. "This ain't about you or whoever you're fuckin' at the time because you know we will fuck you up if you do to Lyssa what you did to Amanda... because this is about our brother. Where the fuck have you been, and why would you bring this April woman here when you knew that Cherie would be here?"

"I didn't know she would be here, Quita. Shit, she ditched him twice already, so—"

"What the fuck is your problem with me?" Cherie sneered. "I didn't do anything to you, but you have an attitude. You did this same

130

shit when I came back home from Cali for my aunt's funeral. Get the shit off your chest 'cause I have to know."

"You really want to know?"

"Yes, nigga, I *gots* to know."

Rich untangled his arm from around Alyssa's waist. He approached Cherie with narrowed eyes. When he was close enough, he pointed at her chest and explained, "My bro has had mental issues since you left, Cherie. Since you left. You would've thought that when you were old enough, you would've found some kind of way to get in touch with him or anybody else. You want to know why and how he has a serious disconnect from the world? It's because of you. To cover up the hurt he was going through, he imagined an entire world that revolved around you. At first, everybody thought that it was cute that he would build a life for you. Then we got to see how serious it was when he had a whole goddamn house demolished just so that he could build you one. Got even more serious when he bought a whole damn wedding set, just by guessing your ring sizes. Was it cute then?" Angrily, he whirled around and eyed each of Shane's sisters. He stopped on Quita, pointing to her. "You want to be mad at me for bringing April? Excuse me for giving him a sense of fuckin' reality; that he could actually live without holding on to a fantasy. And you?" He backed away while eyeing Cherie. "You left again instead of fixing shit. Yeah, I know all about you trying to clear your name and some more shit, but you still forgot about him. You left him drowning inside a fantasy that he couldn't get out of. The nigga committed himself and was locked up inside of a mental institution. Did any of you forget that? It was because he was trying to get out!

April is here because I introduced them to help the both of them. I really don't have to defend myself from either of you. But when my girl called me to let me know about his disconnect, I jump up and come to his rescue while the rest of you are still trying to enable him. You ain't tryin' to help him. You just ridin' the wave, hopin' that it'll be over. Well, it ain't gonna be over. This is the real world!"

Without pause, Cherie took a step and slapped the spit out of Rich's mouth.

When he bounced back, Alyssa caught him, and the rest of the sisters moved in to get ready to rumble if need be.

"Okay, baby," Alyssa said softly, stroking his arm lovingly to get him to calm down.

"Naw, it's not okay. And then y'all wanna question me over Amanda? Y'all need to be askin' how she pushed me over the edge. Y'all think that a nigga is supposed to stick around when y'all bring up bullshit on a regular; when y'all stress him out? Nah. We're supposed to leave before we lose our sanity. Lastly… *Cherie.*"

She didn't like the way he had said her name with so much disgust. She leaned her head over to the side, placing her hands on her hips.

"That's *exactly* what happened to my bro. He was so in love but hurt and confused by everybody dropping like flies or leaving. He didn't want to accept his reality. The delusion and reality clashed. All of you need to understand that shit before you look at me like I'm in the wrong for anything at all. Be mad at yourselves for not helping. What took me so long to get here was the fact that I had to make sure that his business and his money was straight for the next two days. Plus, I was checking up on Miracle at Josiah's; letting him know what was up so that he would keep her a little while longer if need be. You know, doing my motherfuckin' job and duty as the nigga's best friend."

"I think... I think I should go," April mumbled.

"No. Hell no. You're staying until you can get a word with him."

"I think you need to take a little bit of that venom out of your voice," Erykah told him. "We all know that Shane had a mental instability, but excuse the fuck out of us for not pushing it in front of his face. Excuse us for actually living and not leaving him behind because of his mental handicap. What you won't do is stand here and explain shit in front of a basic stranger, putting my brother's business on front street, just because you're bangin' my sister. I know you're his best friend and all, but don't you dare try to tell any of us some shit that we don't fuckin' know. How you handle him and y'all friendship is how you do it. We had different agendas, and we weren't going to constantly remind him that something was wrong. That's straight up bullshit. Now make me tussle with your motherfuckin' ass. Pregnant and all, it can go down. I ain't got no heels or earrings to come up out of, my dude. Catch these hands, homeboy." Erykah stood out of her seat again.

Finally, Cherie spoke up as she slid in front of Erykah. She could feel the woman's rage building. Her heart was heavy, and there was fire brewing in her mouth. "Shane is still able bodied and capable of seeing what's right in front of him. Going to the Pavilion was the best decision he's ever made. By no means were we supposed to write him the fuck off or push him to the side. I know what I did and why I did it, and that's none of your business, *Richard*. Now you done overstepped your boundaries with me one too many times. I don't give a fuck about you being with Alyssa, but what I do care about is you making me out to be a complete bitch. Maybe I was a few times, but it ain't your place to discuss it. Just like you, I don't need to defend myself when we all know what's what. Yeah, I knew that Shane had mental issues, but who the fuck was I to tell him that. He made an adult decision to seek help. He tried to get over whatever poison I had infected him with by trying to replace me."

"Cherie, don't explain yourself to this fool!"

"Oh, no, Erykah, he wanted a discussion, so let me close this out for him. Cherie is a grown ass woman, do you understand that... *Richard*? I'm not somebody's toy to be passed around, and I ain't a topic of fuckin' discussion. Just like you, I was his best friend. Maybe I was supposed to be there to help, but did you forget that I was forced to leave? What did you want me to do? Run away from home and come back to Virginia where I would be dragged right back to wherever the fuck I was at the time, and go to jail as a runaway? Did you want me to leave my abusive boyfriend before he was my even more abusive fiancée, who I was forced into being engaged to just so that my mama could eat and live, only to be dragged right back and have the living shit kicked out of me? You see, Shane ain't the only one who made decisions that he regretted... *Richard*. You need all the facts before you fuckin' come out the side of your neck with shit. It's three sides to every story, and you only saw one. Yeah, I love him. I love him with every-fucking-thing in me, but you're never the one in a relationship with him who has to put up with the jealousy, the reach, the combat, or the insane arguments over something so small. You say you wanted to help with hooking him up with this woman?" She then pointed behind her at April. She waited for him to answer. When he hadn't, she approached April.

April took a sloppy step backward, thinking that Cherie was possibly going to swing at her for no reason at all.

"Nice to meet you, April," Cherie said angrily. "I'm Cherie. I'm his first love and the root to his delusions. Let me give you the rundown, and I don't want no hard feelings when this is over. You see, he tries to find me inside of every female that he's been with. When I look at you, I don't see anything we have in common besides the fact that you're short. He likes his women like that. Good girl. You're off to a good start. Whatever you do with him, always be yourself. If he ever hints at you changing something about yourself, run. Get the fuck away from him. It's because he's going to try to turn you into me. Let's face facts, baby doll. You will never be Rie. You better hold on to Shane and love him your hardest. This is your first hurdle into being with him. And this?" She spread her arms to showcase his sisters scattered around the waiting room behind her. "This is his family. They don't get along all the time, but they stick together. You get slick with them, and they'll wipe the floor with you. They are my girls, but I won't stand in the way of you being with their brother, and neither will they. Shane is always busy working, so don't think he's out cheating. He ain't that. The moment you break his fucking heart, April... You won't have to worry about anybody but me."

"Rie, what are you doin'?" Quita questioned.

She whipped around to Rich to face him. Her jaw flexed. Her

nostrils flared. "I'm letting go," she said through closed teeth. "Like everything else in my life… I'm forced to do so." A stream of tears gently kissed her cheeks.

"Erykah Cruz?" Dr. Wong called.

Her head snapped over to him in the corridor.

"May I have a word?"

She looked back at Cherie and April. Erykah didn't want to hear whatever news it was alone. She knew that Cherie loved her brother with every fiber of her being, but there was a new woman in his life. She hadn't known how close April was with Shane and didn't know if April should've heard of whatever was going on.

"Rich." She huffed as she dropped her head. "Without a fight or argument, please take April back home. I promise to pass the message of what's happening to the both of you."

"What?" he hissed.

"April, I know that you're new, and I will respect the fact that you're his woman, but you don't need to be here right now. I'm trying to protect you from whatever the blow is about to be."

Sadly, April only nodded. "It's nice to have met all of you." Her voice quaked before she dismissed herself.

"Rie… please go and get some rest. Try your best to calm down. You're my sis, and you know I love you, but having him in a hospital bed and having you upset puts a lot of pressure on me. I don't want any of us to stress."

"I'll be back later," she responded gently. Cherie then snatched up her purse that she stuffed her dress and underwear in, picked up her shoes from where she sat, and headed toward the elevator.

With a heavy heart, Erykah dragged herself to the corridor. "What's this about?" she asked Dr. Wong.

He led her to Shane's room, where they had him heavily sedated. Her eyes instantly landed on her brother, lying in his bed, unconscious.

"Ms. Cruz, you are over his estate," Dr. Wong explained. "We have a very serious situation after Dr. Lowe order CT scans and x-rays."

Erykah looked over at the handsome Caucasian doctor who clutched Shane's chart at his side. "What's the problem?"

"Shane has stopped taking his medication. There should be a higher volume of his medicines in his blood and urine work, but there is none."

"He what?" she said with a hiss.

"The only problem, health-wise, that's pulling your brother further and further away from reality is the fact that Dr. Lowe has found an unruptured aneurysm."

The feeling of wanting to puke resurfaced.

"Inside the medial temporal lobe is the region of the brain known as the limbic system, which includes the hippocampus, the amygdala, the cingulate gyrus—"

"Please! Speak *English*."

"The entire temporal lobe controls and processes memory."

"Okay?"

"Your brother's disconnect is medical and mental, simply because he chose to push those hurtful thoughts that we discussed in the institution to the back of his mind. However, he has had this aneurysm for years, and it has gone unnoticed. It's swollen. The medical part of it includes the tumor that Dr. Lowe has found."

"What?" Erykah asked breathlessly.

"Ms. Cruz, the choice is yours to make, since Shane has been medically placed into a coma to suppress the bleeding of his nose," Dr. Lowe informed her. "We're also concerned about an aneurysm that has already ruptured, which explains his nosebleed, thunderous headache, and his nausea. But I must inform you that we have to move quickly."

"Can you remove the tumor and fix his aneurysms?"

"We can. However, with removing the tumor, he might experience memory loss. Some are temporary while others, not so much. He'll have headaches and fits when not being able to recall an event."

"What about his medications?"

"He won't be able to take them," Dr. Wong spoke. "He can have therapy regularly, but no antipsychotics. It may impair his level of thinking. Whereas being in the Pavilion, he could describe plenty of things in great detail, he might not be able to do that any longer after surgery."

"But he won't be mentally retarded either, right? He won't be a vegetable?"

"Not at all. Intelligence comes from the left prefrontal cortex— behind the forehead— the left temporal cortex— behind the ear— and the left parietal cortex, which is at the top-rear of the head. The tumor is beneath that. He'll be fine, Ms. Cruz."

"Do what you need to do then. I can't stand losing my brother, Doctor. We've already lost our father and one of our sisters. The family can't take another loss."

"We have some forms for you to sign, and you also want to go ahead and arrange for the funeral, just in case something happens. There's only an eight percent chance that he won't make it off the table, but it's safer to have brain surgery than it is to fly."

"I'll be back. Have the forms ready for me." Erykah tore away from the room and found the nearest restroom in the hall. She dropped to her knees and let everything spill over into the toilet. She could hold up for others all she wanted, but deep inside, Erykah had crumbled. Shane wasn't there to make her look into his eyes and bear witness to the strength that he was lending her. There was nothing to borrow. She would have to conjure her own strength now.

With a shaky hand, she signed the necessary documents after thoroughly reading over them. Afterward, she kissed Shane's cheek, then curled up on the couch in his room. "You better not die on me, dammit," she mumbled.

Erykah pulled out her cellphone to send text messages, letting everyone know that Shane would be going into surgery in nearly two hours. Everything, like everything else, had fallen pretty quickly. But the young woman sucked up her pride and looked over at her brother when she felt like crumbling again. He wasn't the only one who was tired of losing but trying to live. In no way was she ready to unload it all on him when he was about to walk through fire just to live again.

CHAPTER TWELVE

Play Another Love Song

Cherie's leg danced in the waiting room. She might've told Erykah that she was going to come back, but the truth was that she never left. She sat in her car and remembered that she had an emergency duffle bag in her trunk for if she had to make a run from Terry, the mob or the FBI. She grabbed it come nightfall, strapped it across her torso, then went back up to the floor where they were holding Shane. Cherie went to the restroom to wash up a little, change clothes and to make sure that she was smelling a little better than she did earlier in the day. She had to give Erykah the illusion that she really left. She wasn't going to leave Shane in that building by himself while his sister was already stressing.

She, just like everyone else, had gotten the text message, letting them all know that Shane was going to have surgery in two hours. She hadn't gotten out of the car until it was time for him to head on into the operating room. She had been sitting for close to two hours since then, and she was starting to get nervous.

A thermal cup was held over her shoulder, by a set of pretty coffin nails that she actually admired before she realized that someone was holding out a hot drink to her. "Thank you," she mumbled as she accepted it.

April rounded the set of seats, then sat right next to Cherie. "Herbal tea and honey," she quietly informed her.

"Yeah, you're from Virginia." Cherie giggled before taking a whiff of the tea through the small opening of the top. "We Virginians love our tea."

"Listen, Cherie—"

"April, thank you for the tea… but please don't ruin the moment. I'm tired, stressed and ready to cry like hell right now, alright?"

"I have one of the greatest men on this planet. One of the sexiest specimens to ever want to claim me. He's attentive, supportive, loving… and God, I can't say out loud what else he's talented at, but I'm pretty damn sure you know already. For the life of me, I don't know how one of his exes was highly praised, yet that ex and him didn't work. Rich told me all about your past with Shane—"

"You don't want to fall down that rabbit hole, dear."

"I already have."

Cherie stared at the young woman beside her as she took a moment to sip her tea.

"May Jessica rest in peace," April continued. "Do you know Shane tried to scare me off last night?"

"What?" Cherie's face contorted.

"Yeah." She sighed. April crossed her legs and got a little more comfortable while taking Cherie on a journey that she was not at all expecting. "He started telling me all of this bad stuff about him, which I appreciate the gesture, but I didn't appreciate him trying to push me away. Then I realized, while he was rushing me home, that he's scared. I couldn't quite put my finger on why that was or for what... but he is. After the argument in here earlier, I can see why that is."

"Why is that, April? I told you not to fall down the damn hole, and you *dove* into it."

"Yes, I did. And it's a shame that nobody else realizes what I'm about to tell you. You were all he knew. He basically tried to replace you with Jessica. That was with force. He pushed himself to be with her. Willingly, he gave you a chance. See the difference? Well, hold on for me, beautiful, because it's about to get a hell of a lot deeper." April took a second to sip a little more of her lavender tea, then readjusted herself in her seat so that she could face Cherie. "You were right when you said that I would never be you and that we have nothing in common. Girl, you said yourself that you went through some hellish things. You know what I see? Frickin' Wonder Woman sitting right in front of me. To have the willpower that you do— to come back even though you knew the consequence, and to live a free life, even though it hurts— you're amazing. Me? I'm a damn coward. My family constantly steps on me, and I don't even have the strength, courage, or the balls to speak up for myself, all because I want to keep bullshit down. You and I are polar opposites. Shane knows. That's what scares him. When he forced himself to move on, it was with someone who was a mirrored image of you. Now that he's moving on freely, it's with someone who is nothing at all like you, and it's a fresh start. Very fresh. He's on unfamiliar grounds. You said earlier that you were letting go. I could see the hurt and the pain all over your face because you don't want to let go. And him? He can't find it in himself to see you free."

"April—"

"Cherie, this is bullshit." Her eyes fell upon the arm of the chair. She couldn't look the woman in her eyes. "Don't let him go."

"Excuse me?"

"You're his only constant. If I'm going to be with someone, and I'm going to keep them happy, then I have to do what I have to do. That means keeping you around."

"You have no idea—"

"He is so dependent on you, and I'm trying to see how nobody sees it. He thrives off of you. It's your approval that he thirsts for."

"If that was the case, then why would he try to replace me?"

"It's the same old story. Because you left...I understand why you did, and I'm not going to fault you. I'm not those who have guns blazing because you had to live your life. I, for one, know how it feels to do things that you don't want to for the sake of the family and then have everyone to look down at you for it. I completely understand you, Cherie. I understand the nights you spent crying, wondering when the pain was over, wondering when you were going to be able to go home finally... except your home was long gone. Then you basically end up a prisoner in your own life when you're trying to live it. And then... the one person you love... the one person you count on making everything right...is twisted. He's not like you remember or imagine. Believe me, I understand. Just like I understand that if Shane and I are going to continue, I refuse to do so until you two speak and talk out your problems. I also understand that in the event, he might leave me for you. But you know what? I'm prepared for that. People like us are always prepared for the worst. At least you had someone in your corner who can understand you."

"I can't talk to Shane."

"I want him to be happy, Cherie. I want him to have his friend. Nobody pulls away from reality unless things are truly hard for them. When you left, it was that hard for him… and I know it was even harder for you."

"You realize that he's basically my soulmate, right?"

"That might be true, but I would rather have a happy man at my side than one who isn't all the way there because a part of him is missing."

"You don't understand the magnitude of our relationship."

"I do, and I'm prepared for him to go. I'm used to being left alone. But, the things that Shane has shown me thus far, it's worth me handing him pure happiness on a platter…even if that happiness is you."

"This is crazy," Cherie giggled.

"It is, but love can make you do crazy things. I can't love him fully until you two talk and settle everything. Just like he can't reciprocate said love."

"He's going to leave you, and then he and I won't work."

"If that's the case, push it."

"Girl, you just don't know who I am, do you? Shane and I have been down the road, so I know what to expect."

"Forgive me for not working my neck at you or for picking a fight with my boyfriend's ex. Forgive me for not being combative yet completely honest with you."

"Please."

"So, let's call it a friendly competition then."

"Compete? With me?"

"Yeah. Since me offering you an ally in your corner from the inside of his relationship to help you rebuild your friendship isn't enough for you. Under the condition that you two bury the hatchet, let the best woman win. Hell, I hadn't had to fight, ever. So, this should be interesting."

Cherie studied April's blank face for a second before a smirk pulled across her face. "You must know me better than I thought you did because I enjoy a good challenge."

April knew that she was speaking Cherie's language since she offered up a fight. Cherie was used to having to fight for almost everything she had, and if April and Shane succeeded, then April knew that she would have Shane completely. Not just a piece of him. It was a win-win for everyone.

———————

It took Shane a whole twenty-four hours to open his eyes. When he did, the first person that he had to take the time to focus on was Erykah. She was curled up on the couch in his room underneath her Strawberry Shortcake throw blanket. He reached for his morphine button, knowing that there had to be one near for his headache. Once he found it, he mashed the button in hopes that it would help.

Cherie, in the chair on the opposite side of his bed, heard the beep of the machine and opened her eyes. Her initial thought was that it was his heart monitor, thinking that it somehow flatlined again. She spent many nights waking up in a cold sweat, remembering the sound that made her heart stop.

"Shane," she called him with a raspy voice.

Slowly, he turned his head to see her. She looked beautiful, even though she would've classified herself as a hot mess. Her hair was hiding underneath her silk scarf. Her body was clad in a simple pair of sweatpants and clingy undershirt. He tried his best to keep his eyes on hers as opposed to them being pasted to her breast that were still sitting pretty behind the fabric of her shirt even though they weren't held prisoner in a bra.

"What're you doin' here, Rie?" he quietly asked her. He wasn't sure if she heard him with how quiet he sounded with a dry throat.

Catching the hint, Cherie poured him a cup of fresh ice water then handed it to him so that he could drink it. She waited for him to accept the small pink cup before she relaxed in the hard leather chair with her legs curled underneath her. "Why else would I be here, De'Shane?" she asked him. "You had brain surgery. Am I supposed to be somewhere else?"

He ran his tongue over his teeth and lips before setting the cup down on the table with a slightly shaking hand. "I just figured that..."

"April would be here?"

Shane narrowed his eyes at her. He had never told her about April. "You—"

"Met and spoke with your new girl-toy? Yeah, I did."

"Rie—"

"Look, I'm here for support, okay? I'm not here to fight with anybody. I was worried sick about you, so I never left you."

"So... I did see you before they put me under?" Shane dropped his head then, staring down at the hideous blue covering over his legs and torso. "I thought that was a dream."

"No dream. I was really here. You really called out for me."

"So... I really did have a lobotomy?"

"Technically... yes. They found two aneurysms. One ruptured and one not. They also found a tumor that wasn't helping your insane ass."

"Jokes?"

"Truth. You were out of it for a collective of two days until now."

"And April?"

"She's been here. I'll give her that."

"Nobody disrespected her, did they?"

"No, but Rich got his ass handed to him."

"What?"

"He's dating Alyssa, by the way?"

Shane sucked in a breath to say something, yet the pang in his head reminded him not to get too worked up just yet. He grabbed at his skull, only feeling the bandages that his head was wrapped in. Quickly his anger was replaced with confusion and hurt. He parted his dreads and frantically felt around for a wound or bald spot of any kind.

"Erykah and I have already done that," she giggled. "You only have a quarter of your locs missing. Your scar is in the shape of a question mark. The doctor even said that it would take you a while to get back to normal."

"Normal," he quietly retorted.

"Yeah, but he wasn't talking about your hair."

"What did he mean?"

"Your senses, your language… and you'll sleep a hell of a lot longer than any regular person. He said that you can possibly sleep days at a time."

"What the fuck? Rie, I got to work."

"Don't worry about it. Rich and Alyssa are on it, and you're just going to have to trust them."

"Speaking of them. What else do you have to tell me since you're on a roll? What else did I miss?"

"The fact that Jessica was my sister," she merely whispered.

Shane looked over at her again, but this time it was quicker. It almost gave him a dizzy spell.

"Josiah is my father," she explained. "My mama hid me away on purpose to be petty since he chose his wife and Jessica over her. What a fucked up life, huh?"

"That… that explains why you two looked so much alike."

"Yeah, and it explained the odd connection that me and him had in a jewelry store. Had he not start searching for Davetta to find me, then I wouldn't have known."

"I'm sor—"

"You want to see your scar?" Cherie suddenly perked, to hide her pain. She couldn't hide it from Shane though. He knew her.

She got out of her seat, grabbing her purse from the floor to fetch her compact mirror. Carefully she helped Shane remove part of his bandages so that he could see the staples in his skin that were in the oblong shape of a question mark.

"Shit," he said with a hiss. "This looks like it should hurt a hell of a lot worse than what it actually does."

"It looks gross as fuck, but badass," Cherie commented. "Just don't touch it."

"Evening sleepy head." April appeared in the doorway with a wide smile on her face. Out of the bunch, she was the only one fully dressed. She wore a denim jacket with the sleeves rolled up at the elbows atop a long navy blue maxi dress. Even Cherie had to admire the thin gold belt April wore to complement it.

Cherie stood from the bed as April approached. She placed her large gold purse in the chair that Cherie was going to sit in again, but that was Cherie's cue to leave.

April leaned over and pecked Shane's cheek. "How're you feeling? I didn't expect you to be up for a while."

"Feel like somebody hit me in the head with a hammer," he

answered honestly. "Why weren't you here?"

"Got a call from a guy who was at the Lupus event." April sat on the side of the bed and found the medical tape on the side table so that she could put Shane's gauze back in place. "He wanted to see some more of my work. Had to borrow my sister's car to get there, but I got it done. Had to go to the storage unit to break out a few pieces that I thought that he would love. On top of that, I had to stop being so timid about everything. Almost had a panic attack," she giggled.

"So, what happened?"

"He marveled over them all. He bought all three." Finally finished, she placed her hands on either side of his cheeks. "I'll be the premier artist at his opening in three months."

"Babe... really?" he asked her breathlessly.

"Yes, but I also have some more wonderful news."

"I could use a little more of that."

April took his hands into her own, staring at the covers while readying her words. "I'll be here for the next six days to be with you. I know that Erykah is going to put up one hell of a fight, but I'm prepared for that. If I'm going to be your woman, I can't be meek little April anymore."

"My woman?" Shane paused before looking to his left, finding that Cherie had already vanished. A part of him was heavy, knowing that she had left him there. Why would she just leave? He was silently crying out for her to stay, yet they both knew what would come of it.

"Had a nice conversation with Cherie yesterday, too," April

continued. "I want you guys to talk."

"April—"

"I want you to be happy. Your friend makes you happy. It's just like I told her, I'm willing to accept her in your life. Even though it's a little far, and maybe I'm asking for too much, but it is what it is. I would rather have a happy man than to have one whom I will never have all of. If we're going to be together, then I want all of you."

"I... I don't understand."

"I'm asking you guys to fix your friendship, Shane. You had a disconnect, and there was a reason that you did. According to Rich, it was because she left you. Obviously, you have a void somewhere, and something that you really need to get off your chest. I'm going to need you to speak to her as if you would to me, that way you guys can be friends again. And Shane... don't ever try to push me away again."

"Cherie and I—"

"Are meant to be in one another's lives. It's blatant. We all know, and we can see that. Since you didn't work out as lovers, then that means that you need to patch up your friendship. You have some sort of weird codependency between you two, and I can't see why you keep killing each other like you don't need one another."

"Do you even know what you're even asking me to do?"

"Like I told Cherie, if you're going to leave, at least I know you're leaving for a reason. It won't be because I'm not good enough. It'll be because that's where you truly belong. I'll take purpose over stupidity any day. If nothing happens between you two and you end up with me, then I know that all of you is mine."

"April, I don't want to take you through this."

"Take me through what, Shane? We're not official. We're just having fun. We're only dating. We're still getting to know each other. I would rather you be certain before we go any further than to end up married to you, and wind up divorcing because you call out her name one night in bed."

"I wouldn't do that."

"But we would need to be certain. Do we have a deal?"

"I just had brain surgery, and you're expecting me to make a deal?"

"Yes. Yes, I am. It's either talk to Cherie to mend the past or end up finding you a whole other girlfriend. That's my only request."

He grunted, finally feeling the effects of his morphine. "Fine. But you better not leave me, April. Women have a tendency to find Cherie's presence intimidating, and they leave me."

"Honey… I'm not intimidated. I'm a realist, and I'm an adult. I would rather understand what I'm getting into before I end up with a broken heart."

"Kiss me."

With a smile, April obliged before watching him fall asleep on his morphine. Truthfully, she understood the consequences, and she was down for whatever was about to happen. Shane woke up the woman that she knew was always there, and he was one hell of a man. If it were her chance at real love, then she would take it. If somehow he realized that Cherie was the one, at least April had fun while it lasted. She was only fortunate enough to take her time.

CHAPTER THIRTEEN

Don't Say What You Don't Mean

Six months had gone by before Cherie received a fateful phone call from Shane about their talk. She did well at keeping her distance, even though there was a nagging thought in the back of her mind that told her to claim him before it was too late. The only block was his disconnect. She still felt guilty that it happened to him, and she took full responsibility. To try and erase the thoughts, Cherie hit the gym in her spare time, and she hit it hard.

Reluctantly, Josiah worked out on a regular to keep his diabetes in order and to suppress his cholesterol levels. He and Cherie bonded during that time. They caught up on the darkness that was her life, and he even gave her a little insight on what it would've been like growing up under his roof. He was always hard on Jessica about her grades or about how to earn her allowance. He assured her that Jessica was no princess. She worked for every dime she was given, starting at the age of fourteen. Her cocky demeanor came from her work ethic. It made sense as to why she would throw her car or her credentials in everybody's faces at times. However, the sore that was Davetta hadn't been touched. It was clear why Josiah never chose her, so there was no need in explaining it.

One day, Cherie showed up to Josiah's for a healthy brunch, and Miracle was in a playpen in the living room. Since then, she even had a chance to bond with the pretty little girl. She would play with her every time Miracle was there. She would even go as far as to change her hairstyles since Josiah never would. Surprisingly, Miracle brought a smile to Cherie's face, even though sometimes she would think of Shane and frown. Miracle's glassy eyes would change her facial expression with the quickness. Two months prior, Cherie chatted with Josiah about a decision that was life changing indeed. She asked him about in vitro fertilization. Josiah thought that it would've been a good idea if she could find the perfect donor. Someone healthy, intelligent and handsome. Though it would be a long process, Josiah promised his daughter that she wouldn't have to go through it alone. He would be with her every step of the way.

Today, after staring at herself in the mirror for almost an hour from each side with her stomach poked out, Cherie figured that she would be cute pregnant. It still stung that she wouldn't be having a baby with Shane, but she would have to swallow that and get ready for meeting him.

She dressed in a fitting strapless silk blouse the color of pearl and a pair of black Palazzo pants that damn near covered her black leather peep-toe heels. They complimented the black stones on her blouse for buttons. To set it all off, a black leather choker was around her neck with a small, silver heart-shaped pendant that freely dangled. She grabbed her black leather Coach handbag that she had gotten on sale. Since Royal Six's wasn't really pulling in any customers being that Erykah had yet to open the doors again, Cherie was balling a tight budget. She was only thankful that Davetta's job, along with her savings, was going to keep a roof over their heads, the lights on and food in the kitchen.

Nervousness set in when she pulled up to Apollo's steakhouse and saw the valet out front. Instead of paying ten dollars to have someone else park her car, she saved that cash for gas. She decided to walk so that she could get her head together while doing so. Finally, she ran her fingers through her wavy pixie do that was layered with highlights of blond atop her black tresses. She fingered her long side bangs to make sure that the swoop at the edge of her curls was still cute with her style. When she entered the restaurant, she faced the maître d' with a smile. She pulled off her rose gold Tom Ford shades, then told the woman who she was there to meet.

The young woman led her to the table where Shane was already seated.

As a gentleman, he stood and pulled her chair out for her.

Cherie was in awe at how Shane chose to keep the left, front quarter of his locs cut low over his scar, wearing his dreads up in a sloppy bun. Even apart, they still complimented each other's style. He wore a white button down, pressed black jeans, and black and white Giuseppe sneakers.

"We have to talk about things," he expressed as he took his seat, shutting his eyes tight. "This isn't working. I don't know if I can do this."

"Do what? I just got here." Cherie rolled her eyes.

"I just can't get it off my chest about how we can go over things like adults."

"Let's start with what keeps us going back and forth with the blame."

"No, because we're always going to point the finger, and then you're going to take full blame for everything like you often do."

"Well, if you just stop thinking that you completely know me, then I wouldn't have to shut down an argument."

"That's the thing. We're not supposed to argue. We're supposed to *discuss* things, but we can't," Shane mumbled. "Our discussions always lead to arguments."

"They do."

"Let's clear the air about how I should've manned up and came to find you."

"You had a father to please, De'Shane," Cherie confessed. "You had a whole business that you were getting ready to look after. You didn't have time to come and look for me. Let's be real about it. And even if you did find me, what were you expecting? You were going to get yourself into trouble."

"Maybe so."

"That too is an issue. You think just because you have power then you always have to use it. It was just going to set off a chain of events that neither one of us would've been ready for."

"And?"

"*And* I wish you would stop thinking that everything was going to be happy-go-lucky. Do you know that I was weak as fuck in that house back in Cali? I told you long before I left that I would've died without you. Yeah, well I should've been standing on my two feet. It took my aunt to die for me to make a run for it. You want to know why? It wasn't because I was thinking of Shane. No. It was because I realized how life was too damn short. You want the truth, then there it is. I appreciate the gesture of giving me everything that you thought I deserved, but Shane... I have to get that for me. You lent me strength that I should've been using a long time ago."

"It's too many things that I had to deal with back then," he spoke. "I'm not trying to hurt your feelings, but it's true. You're right, I was too busy. I wish I weren't. Because of it, I had no choice but to hope and pray that you came back on your own. No, I didn't think that you were going to run away, but I did hope that you would've come back to me. Maybe I should've been living a free life, and yeah, I was stuck on you to the point where I pulled away from reality and built a whole world around you. Do you blame me? You were the only sign of peace that I knew. I'm sorry for putting so much pressure on you, Rie. That wasn't my intention."

"The only thing now that we have in common is the fact that we have nothing in common," she confessed. "Shane... I don't really know you like I thought I did. If you asked me anything about your favorites, I wouldn't know."

"Yes, you do. You just don't know it."

"There's the acceptance again."

"What are you talking about? When did the *acceptance* thing happen the first time?"

"Shane." Cherie huffed, leaning forward to deliver some heavy news that she was sure to get out into the air to make him understand. "When I left, you couldn't accept that. It was that and the fact that you had to leave Michelle. Shortly after, she passed away. You were then introduced to a whole other family. Everything happened so quickly. You refused to accept that, so you pulled away from what was real. I was the root of all that shit, and while I forgive you for the so-called pressure, I'm the last thing that's still here, detouring you from your reality."

"What are you saying?"

"I'm saying that I can't let you do this anymore." The tail-end of her sentence was barely audible. She was choking up. The tears were threatening to spill over. "I'm poison for you."

"No." Slowly, Shane shook his head.

"Yes, and I can't kill you anymore."

"Listen to yourself for a second."

"I am the person who kills you and gives you life all the same. That's not healthy."

"Stop." Shane clenched his jaw. At that very moment, she was killing him.

"You have a very good woman at your side—"

"Stop it, Mon Cherie."

"You have to treat her right. Treat her like you would treat me."

"Stop running away from me." His teeth were clenching so hard that he was afraid that she wouldn't have been able to hear him.

"I'm not running, dammit. I'm giving you a chance to live. That woman wanted us to patch up our friendship, but you know what happens between us. This spark happens, and then we're in love before everything collapses altogether."

"You are running—"

"I am not going to be held responsible for April's heartbreak when that spark presents itself, do you understand? You're already falling for the woman. So fall peacefully, purely and unjustly."

"Rie—"

"Shane... no matter where you go..."

"No—"

"No matter where you are..."

"Don't use my own words on me."

"No matter what you do... I will always be there with you."

"This is bullshit. You know that I love you."

"This is the downfall of you. How in the hell can't you see that?"

"Because where you may see nightfall as darkness, I see it as the nocturnal's time to play." He had to take a step back to show her the metaphorical side of him that she hadn't seen in a while. Maybe that would show Cherie that he was still there. "My downfall, as you call it, is something painfully beautiful. How can you willingly to leave me again?"

"It's going to be a merry-go-round, and we need to get off it."

"Do you know that my sisters have been working around the clock in the last six months to make sure that everything within my home was straight? They've been waiting on me hand and foot? I can't even shoo April away. I've had speech therapy, physical therapy, still had to work here and there, and take care of my daughter. Where the hell were you?" Shane's anger was rising. He was going to have to suppress it before his head reminded him of why he couldn't be angry. "It's fine. I can't make stop you from leaving when you're already gone."

Shane stood and looked down at her. She looked like one hell of a strong woman, but she still wasn't the Cherie that he remembered. She was a mirage. After all of the years that he thought of her or felt that he knew her, it was evident that he didn't. In the matter of fifteen seconds of standing over her, he came to the conclusion that letting go would be best. Neither of them could live while holding on to one another. Whereas it would've bothered him before his surgery, it didn't now. Shane had learned, after his release, to appreciate the smaller things and to not push the subject of the word "no." Thanks to his lobotomy, this was a lot easier than he ever imagined it would be. He swallowed his pride and did something that he never thought he would.

Contrary to the other time that he said it before Jessica was gunned down, he actually meant it this time with a heavy heart and aching spirit. "Goodbye, Cherie. Take care of yourself."

With that, he turned away to leave, holding his head high. He still couldn't fight the fact that he knew her so well. He knew that she was crumbling inside and she was burning just like he was.

Cherie waited for him to exit, sipped from the water that was sitting on the table, and threw on her shades so that she could get to her car with what little dignity that she could muster. Purposely, she cut out a piece of her own heart and watched it walk away from her. With pride in her step, she reached her car and hurriedly got inside. No matter how either of them held their heads high and marched as if they hadn't been damaged, both of them broke once inside their vehicles. For Shane, it was resting his head back on his headrest while his tears left a hot trail to his ears. With Cherie, she had to press her forehead against her steering wheel, clutching it for dear life. She let out some of the most hurtful screams when realizing what she had done. She almost broke a nail with how she banged her fist against the tight leather of her wheel. Cherie convinced herself that what she had done would benefit him more than it ever had.

The very next day, inside of her dark bedroom, Cherie received a phone call that made her hop out of bed and scurry out of her apartment in her pajamas. Shane, however, was already out working at high noon. He called April to relay the message. Even though she was covered in paint, she obliged and took the 2018 black on black Cadillac Deville that she picked out months ago for her birthday that Shane surprised her with. When she arrived in the parking lot, a not so glamorous woman stepped out of a Ford next to her. April readily identified her as Cherie but wondered why she looked like shit. Cherie, in turn, snarled at her internally.

They had to remember that they were called to the hospital for a reason. Together, they located the elevator and used the directions that they were given. Cherie, a step ahead of April, turned into the room first. Her eyes landed on Shane in the chair beside Erykah's bed, holding an infant. The smile on his face as he spoke to his nephew gut-punched her. It knocked the wind out of her.

"Look at him," April happily sang as she swayed over to Shane. "He's so darling."

"Rie," Quita giggled from behind her.

She moved aside to let her into the room.

"I forgot our sashes."

"Sashes?" Cherie quizzed.

From Quita's hands, she passed out pink silk sashes that read "Auntie" on them. She gave one to Alyssa, Ashington, and then one to Cherie. Hesitantly, she took it.

"Thank you," she mumbled.

"Now, the baby shower is two weeks from now, since we know now that he's a boy."

The toilet in the bathroom flushed, then Erykah emerged from it with Joyce helping her to the bed. "His name is King," Erykah told them all. "King Sabti Cruz. Y'all wanna fight about it?"

"If you don't sit your sore tail down somewhere," Quita told her. "You can't fight now."

"Don't pick on her, Marquita," Joyce warned her. "I do not want these stitches to pop if she gets mad at you."

"Girl, where is your catheter?"

"She didn't want one," Ashington spoke up from the countertop that she was sitting on, with Miracle in her lap. "You should've seen her fighting the nurses when they were trying to give her anesthesia."

Erykah smacked her teeth. "They weren't gonna try to dope me up, then trick me by switching my baby at birth. Hell naw. So when he grows up and gets into some trouble, I have the right to complain about the labor and the pain."

"Was it a hard birth?" Cherie quizzed.

Erykah eyed her while trying to adjust herself in her bed. "Why? You got somethin' you want to tell us?"

"No," she giggled. "I just want to know. I don't know anybody who's had babies recently."

"Actually, it was like he screamed at the last minute that he was ready to be here. Before they could get me on a bed, he was already crowning. Soon as they gaped me open, he was sliding right out. It was scary, I can tell you that. I thought that I was going to split open, but I knew that I had to forget about my pain to get him here. It was actually beautiful, though. Now, Shane, give me my baby."

"Oh, naw." He quietly chuckled. "You remember what you said about Miracle? That she was going to be passed around? Yeah, ditto, Rick."

"That wasn't me, that was Quita."

"Well, sisters of a feather."

"Mama," she groaned.

"Shane," Joyce sweetly called him. "Hand your nephew over."

"Yeah, hand him right over to me." Quita bent at the waist to take little King into her arms.

"I should've been the only child," Erykah complained.

"Unfortunately, that was not in daddy's plans. I'm surprised he didn't catch nothin.'"

"Don't speak about my husband like that," Joyce shrieked. "He made his mistakes, yes, but y'all were blessings."

"Listening to Erykah scream like that, it's no wonder our mamas were mad." Ashington cackled. "To go through all that pain and present a baby to a man who didn't want them must've been hard."

"Tell me about it. Bringing life into this world isn't easy. And sometimes living life itself ain't easy either. Still, your father loved all of you equally."

"Somebody ain't feeling this."

Everyone took their sights to Ashington, watching Miracle squirm against her and clench her neck tightly.

"I guess she just figured out that she's not the baby anymore. Thank God I don't have any replacements. I would act just like her."

"Girl, shut up," Alyssa finally spoke from the chair she sat in, in the far corner of the room. "I thought that our clan stopped at Jazz and me. But nooo, you just had to pop your little ass up."

"Right," Quita laughed. "Lyssa was the baby until you showed up."

Ashington rolled her eyes. "Not my fault that our daddy was a…" She looked over at Joyce then and shut off her sentence completely.

"Rie?" Erykah called her. "You want to hold your nephew?"

"I... actually... ummm..." Cherie fidgeted with her sash for a moment, trying to come up with an excuse.

"Girl, don't act like you ain't family," Alyssa said. "You standin' all the way over there by the door like you're a visitor. What's up? You got me over here thinkin' that you want to make a run for it."

"No... I just... umm..."

"Rie got baby fever." Ashington snickered.

"Come talk to mama." Joyce rubbed Erykah's shoulder before leaving.

"Oh, no," Cherie opposed. "I'm fine."

"You can't lie to me girl. I done been there and done that. Let's go."

Erykah waited for the women to leave and close the door before her head whipped over to her brother. She didn't care if April was sitting there or not. She was going to make her point. "What the fuck did you do?" she asked through gritting teeth.

His face contorted. "Why I had to do something?"

"Because she's broken. Nothing breaks Cherie but Shane."

"Hello," Quita commented with her eyes on her nephew.

"What did you do?"

Shane rolled his eyes. "All I did was give her what she wanted. She thought it was best for us to part ways. I gave it to her."

"Why do y'all insist on killin' each other? I have no clue, but I'm done with it. If y'all can't see it then fuck it."

"It was *my* idea," April suggested.

"Listen, I like you. I really do. Thank you for making my brother happy and all… but some things shouldn't be touched, and that's one. It's like an antibiotic and infection. You fix one of them then you break the other. The next time you feel like fixin' something, you need to closely analyze the situation. This is one situation that has been analyzed, and it's a difficult equation to solve. Nobody on the outside can fix whatever has been fucked up between them."

"We've tried," Quita remarked.

"Just don't touch it."

"Excuse me," April choked. She got up to leave. She thought she was helping, but apparently, she made things worse.

Shane followed to try and catch her.

Both of them whisked past Joyce and Cherie in the hall, and Cherie couldn't help but watch them as they bolted toward the elevator.

"Talk to me, Mon Cherie," Joyce urged her. "What's on your heart?"

"I got to get out of here," she confessed. "Sometimes I wish I just would've stayed away to keep everything down, you know?"

"But why?"

"I didn't have a choice by to leave because I was a minor. It's just… complicated. He would've had a disconnect, but maybe a good girl would've come along and helped him come back to the real world. I just had to show up to ruin everything."

"Cherie, are you blaming yourself for everything?"

"I don't have a choice."

"The situation is a shitty one, but you know what we do?" Joyce placed the tip of her pointer finger underneath Cherie's chin to bring her line of sight up to her eyes. "We push on, and we live. You're still young, eligible, beautiful… you just need to live for Cherie. It ain't gonna be easy, ya' hear? But let me tell you, baby girl. What's meant for you will always come back around." She took a moment to flash her wedding set at Cherie. "I've had to watch a man create kid after kid, and I thought that it's what would've been best for him; to be free. What I didn't know until after we were married was that he lived with the haunting thought of what could've been between us. I was the only woman that he was willing to commit to. Apollo was all about Joyce. You know how many times I had to move to keep him from putting money in my mailbox, scaring off potential lovers or from showing up with a bouquet of roses? But you have to believe me when I say that there was a gleam of hope and desperation in his eyes once we saw each other face to face after twelve years. I knew he wasn't going to stop approaching me, but he surprised me by only asking about Erykah. Blew me completely away that he didn't try to woo me. But you listen to what I say, Mon Cherie. Matter of fact, you say it to me. Tell me that you believe that what's for you will be there."

She sniffled. Cherie hated to cry in front of other people, yet her heart didn't care about her pride. "What's for me will be there."

Joyce wrapped her arms around Cherie to give her yet another motherly hug that she hadn't ever received from Davetta. She sank into it and simply enjoyed it instead of only receive it.

Letting go hurt a hell of a lot worse than she thought it would be. She was prepared for pain but not as much as she was getting at the moment.

CHAPTER FOURTEEN

Sugarcoated Wounds

To celebrate Miracle's first birthday, Shane pulled out all the stops. There was a petting zoo, clowns, ponies, and he even rented a mansion that had a pool in the back so that all of his employee's kids could come out and celebrate in style. Cherie reached out to Joyce about it, and when Joyce told her that she was more than welcome to help, for some reason, Cherie jumped at the chance. In her mind, since she was planning for a baby, she might as well get used to things like that. Though she only saw Shane in passing, it was obvious to everyone that they chose to make each other invisible. The two didn't share a word in passing or eye contact. It was deeper than everyone thought. Even to April. She didn't open up about it since Erykah basically told her to keep her mouth closed.

The little princess had loads of gifts that she probably wasn't going to bang against the floor. Cherie almost cried when Shane held her up in front of a three-tier cake to showcase her short-sleeve onesie and her bejeweled tutu that Erykah personally designed. Miracle was not only her niece but a symbol of what could've been and what was possibly to come for her.

Days later, Cherie found herself sitting in her doctor's office, waiting for a batch of good news. She actually received it. Her doctor told her that she was fertile enough being that she had been taking the pills that he prescribed to her. She had already found a donor inside a handbook that was provided to her after her second visit. The only thing to stop her when she got the green light, was the thought of her not having this moment with Shane. Josiah, sitting right next to her, squeezed her hand when he saw the look on his daughter's face. Joyce, sitting on the other side, rubbed her back for comfort. They had too much in common for her not to understand the squeeze of Cherie's heart when she was told that she could have a baby with any man in the catalog that she had gone over plenty enough times that she could remember all 200 pages of potentials.

"Thank you," she politely told the doctor from the opposite side of his desk. "I will reach out to you when it's time to knock me up."

He only nodded to dismiss them all.

"Are you ready for this, Pumpkin?" Josiah asked her as he escorted her out of the building. "You know, there is no rush in doing this. You can always hold off for a few years."

"Dad... seriously... I have to do this for me," she stressed. "I mean, look at us. The both of you. I love the both of you unconditionally, and I recently met you. I want that kind of love. Someone who can't just up and leave me. Someone who can possibly break my heart but heal it with an accomplishment. Finally, I want to be a better mother than my own."

"Cherie, honey," Joyce called out to her. "I'm behind you in whatever you decide to do. If you have it all figured out, then by all means, go for that leap. However, I don't advise you to make this decision prematurely. We can't return children."

"Tell me about it," Josiah commented. "There were plenty of times I wanted to find the receipt for Jessica to give her back."

"Oh, my Erykah was no different. That girl had a hard head and was as stubborn as a mule. Many nights I had to sip brown liquor in my tea, to keep from bashing her damn skull in."

"Don't talk about my sisters," Cherie said with a giggle. "This is what I want. I'm very sure of it."

"Then we'll call your doctor on Monday morning and book your first appointment."

"A strapping grandson shouldn't be too hard for you to make, would it?" Josiah joked.

"Daddy, really?" Cherie raised a brow at him.

"Well, I already have a dainty little princess. Why not hope for a football or baseball star from you?"

"Can we go and eat please?" Cherie wiped away what little tears streamed down her cheeks with a smile. With Josiah and Joyce, she felt more love than she ever had. A baby within that would make her complete.

When she had gotten into her car, she did something that she never thought of doing. She pulled out her phone when weighing the options of having to wait for an appointment and the benefits of getting man juice on her own. Cherie waited for the line to stop ringing as she arranged her words carefully.

"Hello?"

"Damon," she greeted him. "Hey, ummm… I was on the way to get something to eat with my honorary mom and my dad. I was wondering if I could stop by."

"Why would you be stopping by?"

"You're going to think I'm crazy, but it benefits you a lot more than you think. Just… one screw for the road? Please?"

"Do you know how long it's been? And you decided to hit me up for what?"

"To clear the air… and to… Look, I'll explain when I get there okay?"

"Leave your bullshit in your car before you come up, alright?"

"See you soon." Cherie hung up with her heart pounding. Was she making a mistake?

———

Months ago, April walked into Shane's rented home expecting to cook. However, she walked into him standing in front of the dining room table with candles lit around the room. He was dressed in a pressed white polo and starched jeans. Against his palm, he was tapping a velvet box there, and the look on his face said that he had something very important to ask her. She tried her best to talk about the food that she wasn't sure he cooked himself on the table behind him, but he carried on with his speech to get his point across. The ending result was April crying and breathlessly telling him that she would marry him.

Just now, she decided to tell her family about her engagement, and Shane shocked the family when he told them about his engagement. His sisters gave him all the flack that he could imagine, especially by bringing up the point that April was weak and that she wouldn't have been able to sustain his work ethic. Still, he helped to plan his own wedding. His sisters pushed their egos and anger to the side to help him since they were told that April really had no one. Besides, they didn't want it to look a mess. Personally, he was flying out members of his family from Michelle's side that he knew so that they could celebrate. Apollo's side only enjoyed the fact that they were being housed and fed for free.

Cherie, however, received her invitation from Erykah. Sadly, but surely, she handed it over to Cherie and urged her to be her plus one to the ceremony. She knew that Cherie would have a raving fit, but she hoped that it would at least make her open her eyes to see that she belonged with her brother. Honestly, the only reason April accepted the proposal in the first place was to make Cherie spring out of the woodwork to scream out how she couldn't live without Shane. Fatal mistake. Cherie hadn't budged in three months since receiving word that Shane was getting married. She resorted to old habits of swallowing it, closeting the pain, and pushing forward. She had a baby to plan for. April was going to have to live that lie by her-damn-self.

Knowing that the time for Shane to marry was strongly approaching, Cherie had to get out of the house and take a walk through downtown Richmond. She thought of Joyce telling her that if it's meant for Shane to marry April, then it would happen. Joyce was even honest enough by telling Cherie that she knew Shane would get cold feet at the last minute. She had to remind Cherie that Shane was Apollo's son. He was stubborn, but he would come to his senses. That's not what Cherie wanted to hear. It only hurt to know that he had gotten the baby without her, and now he planned an entire wedding that didn't consist of her at all. But this was what she wanted, right? To let him go off and live without the so-called poison that was her. That's what he was doing. It was like slicing her open with razors and holding her down in a tub full of rubbing alcohol.

Simply dressed in a pair of over-the-knee heeled boots, skin-tight jeans and clinging long-sleeve white shirt, she clutched her purse in her hands in front of her. Finally, she found a nice place where she could eat. The Roosevelt.

As soon as she placed a foot on the first step, a crowd of men poured out of the door, cheering and raving about strippers. One, in particular, stood out to her. The men had given him a scepter and a golden crown. She had to admit that he wore it well, but it wasn't for her. Cherie pushed on, saying her excuses to the gentlemen that she shimmied through. She needed a drink.

Shane knew that voice even in his sleep. He turned to see only the back of her briskly walking through the restaurant to get to the bar. She wanted him to live. Like every other request of hers, he had to oblige. Shane gulped and turned away. He adjusted the crown on his head, then proceeded to the line of three party buses that pulled up for him.

It wasn't until he was seated in front of a curvy, half-naked specimen on the bus that he cried out inside again of how desperately he wanted Cherie to do something. Call him tonight, maybe, and tell him to stop the charade. Give him permission to take off his mask and love her the way that he was struggling to love April.

———————

The women, across town, were seated inside April's suite, drinking wine and champagne. Erykah was already uncomfortable, seeing as how Ashington was alone with King and Miracle. She knew the two would run over Ash. Other than that, she didn't like the venom and hatred in Nicola's eyes every time April opened her mouth to say something. Quita constantly had to remind her that this was not her party and that she was going to have to let April stand up for herself.

"Any advice?" April asked the women with a smile.

"Yeah, don't live a lie," Nicole commented before sipping from her glass.

"Girl, if you ain't got nothin' nice to say then you need to shut the fuck up." Surprisingly, it wasn't Erykah's mouth that everyone heard. Alyssa stood from the couch next to her sister, on bare feet, scowling at the woman across from her.

"Alyssa," Joyce lovingly called her.

"Nah, ma. She been cuttin' her eyes at April since we were at dinner. We're Cruz's. We don't do that secret hate shit for our own. I'm real allergic to this bitch right now. I need her away from me."

"Who the fuck are—" Nicola challenged as she rose from her seat, only to be sat right back down by Quita.

"Nuh-uh, sugar lump. You might want to sit right back down. This girl might look like she got some sense, but umm… she's a savage."

"When I talk to my sister, then that's just it!"

"Who you raisin' your voice at?" Erykah asked her. "Now whatever issues you got with April, then you should've left that at the door. You can't so-call celebrate with somebody and sit over there in your feelings. That ain't how we do things. She's about to be a Hartford-Cruz. That means she's in our family, no longer in yours. You need to get some act right before her sisters-in-laws have to start snatchin' weave."

"And if you got enough disrespect to put her down on her special day, then you really don't need to be around us," Alyssa finished. "Smile and be fuckin' merry before you end up dragged up out this motherfucker."

"April?" Nicola called to her. "You're just going to sit there while they verbally abuse me?"

"Did you defend me when Tucker threw insults at me?" she countered. "Did you even think to open your mouth to tell him to knock it off? Did you care about how it hurt me?"

"Oh, so she's a weak bitch?" Alyssa tilted her head over while staring at Nicola.

"She needs a lesson in sisterhood for real," Quita said with a laugh. "I'll be damned if a man gon' talk to my sister any kind of damn way."

"What daddy said?" Erykah asked her.

"The bigger they are, the harder they fall. Got me fucked up."

"Get your shit, Becky," Alyssa announced to Nicola, snapping her fingers at the woman. "Get your shit and get out of the suite that April's man paid for."

"I'm not going anywhere." Nicola worked her neck at Alyssa.

Joyce reached out to gently touch Nicola's arm from where she was sitting. "Sweetheart, it's best that you just leave. I can't control all of my daughters at once. You're just going to have to come to the wedding."

"April?"

"Bye, Nicola," April said softly with her eyes on the marble coffee table in front of her.

"You are so wrong for this," she mumbled. She grabbed her purse from the floor, then scurried into the master's suite to retrieve her duffle bag that she packed for the night. When she left, the front door thundered off.

"We don't care about you slammin' doors, either!" Alyssa shouted. "Gon' purposely try to ruin somebody's day. Fuck out of here."

Joyce stood and took notice of the only three cousins that April invited to what was supposed to be her bachelorette party, sitting at the bar near the kitchen of the suite. "Does anyone else want to leave? You're more than welcome to do so."

"Y'all wasn't gon' take up for your family?" Quita asked over her shoulder.

"Fuck her," one young woman said. "She's been a bitch to April since—"

"No!" April shouted. "Shut up!"

"You might as well get it out into the air. These people need to know why she's such a bitch."

"April, honey?" Joyce cooed. "You got somethin' you want to say to mama?"

"Girl, you might as well," Erykah said. "She's gonna hit you with the sweet voice, and it's gonna make you cry and surrender."

April stood and straightened her clinging white dress, then fidgeted with her sash that let others know that she was a bachelorette. "My father was a deacon, yes," she began. "But he wasn't the most perfect father, alright? He would call me bad names when he was drunk. One day, when everyone was away, he said that it was… it was time to see what a woman I was. But… I knew that he was drunk, so I didn't say anything. When I finally spoke up… everybody called me a liar. Nicola blames me for our parents' divorce and the fact that he was demoted in the church because of his perversions."

"That wasn't your fault," another cousin spoke up. "You know that, and you need to live with it. And it's still no reason for her to toot her nose up at you. She's stupid. I don't blame them for putting her out."

"Honey, I'm sorry," Joyce lovingly said as she embraced her. "You were brave enough to speak up. That makes you a winner."

"Yeah," April sniffled. "So, I just stopped standing up altogether after that. I lost my sister in the mix."

"That bitch been gone," Quita assured her.

"Through drugs, prostitution and other foolishness, I never lost my sisters," Alyssa informed her while she was still being hugged by Joyce. "Matter of fact, come and hug me, dammit! I ain't hugged y'all since Daddy's funeral."

Quita and Erykah laughed at her, but they shared a family moment where they embraced their sister.

April wouldn't mind being in a family that genuinely loved and cared for one another, but it wasn't her place to be there. She knew so.

CHAPTER FIFTEEN

I'm Here On The Edge

Cherie's thoughts weren't on her making her baby. Her mind was on how hard she would have to scrub her skin to get the imaginary dirt off. She avoided Damon's lips when he tried to give her a peck on the cheek before she left his apartment at almost three in the morning. Honestly, she thought that she would stay and have him distract her from the fact that her soulmate was getting married in nine hours. To no avail. She hated everything about Damon and even more so, everything about herself.

Damon leaned against the pain of his front door shirtless. Even his chiseled physique did nothing for her. "You sure you want to leave?" he lowly asked, after running his tongue across his thick lips. "We can crack open another bottle and—"

"No, it's fine," she mumbled. "I just really need to go home and get some sleep."

"You know you said that we can't contact each other after this, remember? So why not stay a little longer?"

"I just..." She came close to telling him the real, about how she didn't want to be near him, and how she didn't want to wait on appointments just to succeed at conceiving. Instead, she confessed, "I was using you, and I don't feel right about it."

"But I'm enjoying it." He presented that smile of royalty that she used to love, but it also didn't move her.

Cherie caressed his cheek with somber-filled eyes. "Goodbye, Damon," she quietly announced.

He watched her walk away and felt almost nothing besides anger. He couldn't see how someone that beautiful and hard-working would settle for someone who was basically dragging her along. He just didn't understand the connection.

———————

As Cherie walked up the steps to her condo, she had the eerie feeling that she was being watched. She constantly looked over the shoulder of her jacket to see if someone was there, but she didn't find anyone with prying eyes. Maybe it was Shane, wanting to desperately say something to her. She wasn't in the business of stopping what seemed like true love. Especially seeing as how April got the ring before she did. She was still bitter about that, but she kept in mind that she was having a baby. Surely it would mask all of the other bullshit, right?

"Cherie?" a voice called to her.

She stopped at the top of the stairs and turned. Through narrowed eyes she saw Davetta waddling towards the stairs. "Where the hell are you coming from at this time of night?"

Davetta gripped the rail to step up on the first stair with a grin on her face. "Terry came by to see you, but you weren't—"

"*Terry?*" Her face contorted.

"Yea, he just pulled off."

"Davetta, how the hell does Terry know where we live?"

"He called me up and said that he wanted to talk. He said that he missed you, Rie."

"Terry doesn't miss me. He's engaged to Roxanna."

Davetta's head tilted to the side. "That fat ass girl that was married to Marcus Calhoun?"

"Yea, her. Mama, I don't want you seeing Terry anymore. Got it?"

"It was innocent," Davetta returned with a giggle.

"Ain't shit ever innocent with Terry or his damn daddy, and you know it. Don't contact him again."

"Fine." Davetta huffed as she carried herself up the stairs.

Cherie watched her closely, noticing that her mother was drunk. Terry must've gotten her inebriated on purpose to try and get some information out of her. Hopefully Davetta didn't give him any.

Her assumptions were wrong when she received a text that told her of how beautiful she still looked from behind. She set him straight and let him know not to contact her again. Afterward, she blocked Terry from calling or texting. She had other things to worry about than that of Terrance— the man who was nothing that he presented himself to be when they were dating. She had to get ready to put on a brave face so that she could watch the other half of her heart walk down the aisle and claim someone else in a few hours.

Shane, at four in the morning, sat out in the driveway of his home that he had built for Cherie, with a cigarette between his lips. He was sitting on the hood of his Jaguar, trying to clear his thoughts. All of his guests were sound asleep after getting drunk and loving the dancers who were relentless with robbing them by using their mounds and jiggling flesh. He put on the best mask that he could to make it seem as if he was really enjoying himself. Now that he was mere hours away from taking April's hand, he had a lot more thinking to do. He had a solid opportunity to turn away from his band of men at the Roosevelt, grab Cherie by the waist and tell her that he didn't want to marry April, yet he didn't take it. He was too far in for turning back now.

As he released a cloud of smoke from his lungs, a set of headlights turned the corner near his home and parked right in front of him. It couldn't have been Cherie. She didn't drive a luxury coup. It damn sure wasn't April, because the car she drove was Cadillac. This car was a Jaguar, the same as his, only an older model. Shane didn't even bother to shield his eyes from the lights before the driver shut them off.

Out of the coup stepped a tall and athletically fit man, simply dressed in a pair of sweats and a t-shirt. The man that he didn't have a problem assaulting in a church parking lot, or the man he stalked to make sure that Cherie would stay safe from harm while she was away from him.

"Too early for you to be lurkin', ain't it?" Shane asked Terry. He pulled from his cigarette as Terry approached him.

"Not really. Had to pay you a visit. Had to come and see how you live since it was real cool for you to drop by my shit. I didn't expect for you to be up, but I guess that's a plus."

"So, what? If I was upstairs, in my bed, what were you gonna do? Just stand out here and watch my house?"

"Most likely." Terry nonchalantly shrugged.

"Bad idea, my brotha. You see, unlike you, my house is a fortress. I would've reviewed the tapes from my security cameras and would've seen you. So, what's the real deal? Why're you here?"

"Heard you got yourself into a little predicament. You're getting married tomorrow, aren't you? And it ain't to my Cherie."

"Let's get two things straight... *brotha*." Shane took another pull off his cigarette to try and keep his anger at bay. It was clear that Terry was only there to push his buttons. "I don't care how you know where I live, because this ain't my only spot. Secondly, she ain't *ever* been your Cherie."

"Me having her virginity tells me a completely different story."

Shane burst into laughter, so much so that his shoulder shook and a tear spilled over. He swiped it away from his cheek with the knuckle of his pointer finger. Shane tried to get his breaths in order before he spoke.

"What the fuck is so funny?" Terry asked angrily.

"Is that what she told you? That she was a virgin? Or is that what you *assumed*?"

"Fuck you mean?"

"Terry," Shane chuckled. "Oh, boy." He took time to thump

his ashes. "Let me tell you a short story about the woman that you obviously don't know how you think you do. She had an abortion in her teens because her mama's sorry ass boyfriend raped her. That alone should tell you that she was nowhere near a virgin when you got to her. Lastly, Cherie lost her virginity at age twelve, nigga. I should know because *I'm* the one to claim it."

"Low life ass dude." Terry snarled.

"Says the motherfucker who came all the way out here from Cali to stalk a woman who moved on damn near two years ago. Oh, and he decided to watch a whole other grown man's house because he thought said grown man was asleep. You real funny. But..." Shane shrugged as he pulled again from his cigarette. "I guess it's easy to assume she was fresh, because that pussy locks tight when I slide off in it." Shane blew his smoke into Terry's face.

"Moral of the story, I still get Cherie. You don't. Enjoy your wife now. Leave Cherie alone, De'Shane."

"Terry. Don't you *ever* roll up on me like a motherfucker like me will ever be afraid of you. Watch yourself. You might not wake up the next time you think you can intimidate a fool like me."

Terry started to return a quip until he had the urge to turn his head to his left. A red light almost blinded him until he focused and noticed Rich on the porch of Shane's home, holding a gun steady in one hand and a blunt in the other. The laser beam on the head of the gun was pointed directly between Terry's eyes.

"Anything else you want to tell my patna?" Rich asked him.

Terry was furious. He ground his teeth so hard that he almost cracked them. Instead of saying another word, he returned to his Jaguar. He stopped when he reached for his handle and looked at Shane with a smirk on his face. "Wouldn't it be a shame if the feds found out about your little operation? It's a pity how your old man left you with such a large cartel without knowing that it would one day crumble."

"Homeboy, I ain't scared of your threats," Shane returned. "I'm a goddamn god. I have more reach and more connections. Whatever you want to throw at me, I can handle it. Now go on and cry in the car over a woman who still don't want your ass."

Terry snatched open the car door to leave, but Shane had one more little piece of information for him.

"Oh, and Terrance... if you decide to fuck with Cherie, whether she's with me or not... I'm comin' to see you personally. No if, ands, or buts about it." Finally, Shane thumped his cigarette butt and slid off the hood of his car. "Get the fuck off my block in that old ass excuse for a Jaguar. You damn sure ain't gonna get Cherie back in that piece of shit."

Rich held the beam on Terry until he pulled off. When Shane was close enough, he handed him the blunt so that he could get a nice long inhale of something to calm him down. "You want to talk about it?"

"Same old shit. Nigga wants to intimidate me over Rie. Then he brought up the fact that I'm getting married. I want to put his ass to sleep."

"Wait until he tries to strike," Rich offered. "If Apollo were here, he wouldn't have found anything he said to you as a serious threat. The dude's a fuckin' coward. You know that. Wait until he tries to grab his balls, and then cut 'em the fuck off. If not, Apollo would've called it wasted blood."

"You right." Shane choked on the chronic that Rich had given to him.

Rich patted his back to help him breathe for a moment. "Damn, dude! You ain't smoked in a while, huh?"

"Fuck you, Rich," he choked.

"Let's get you back in the house so you can get married tomorrow. Don't worry about him, Cherie, or nothin' else. You got to think for Shane."

Little did Rich know, it was much easier said than done.

EPILOGUE

Something Like Heaven, But More Like Hell

"Shane, be the hell still," Erykah complained as she straightened his bowtie. "It's going to be crooked, and you're going to look a mess."

A knock came at the door, and all hearts stopped momentarily, thinking that it was Mama J coming to give Shane his kisses before he took his trip down the aisle. The siblings prayed that she could talk some sense into him before he met April at the altar. However, it was not. With a slumped and saddened demeanor, Quita pulled the door open and stepped aside so that she could let Joyce's sister Ethel into the chambers.

Erykah rolled her eyes. She couldn't stand her old aunt. The woman was tipsy already. She stumbled over her four-inch heels to meet her honorary nephew before he could marry. Her frumpy body pressed into his when she hugged him, and even he had to pull his head back to avoid the sting of his nostril when inhaling the liquor on her breath.

Politely, Quita escorted her back to the door so that she could take her seat. "You better know… you're making a mistake," Ethel slurred. "That girl ain't in love with you, and you ain't in love with her. You're doing this for nothin.'"

"Alright, Aunt Ethel," Erykah said dryly. "Go on and take your seat."

As soon the door closed, Shane whipped away from Erykah and dove over to the side of the couch that Rich was sitting on to a wastebasket there. Rich continued to shine Shane's dress shoe in his hand while his friend upchucked.

"So, it's clear that I don't have to tell you that you're nervous as fuck, right?" Rich asked him.

Shane slowly turned his head to look at him through narrowed eyes.

"I don't blame you, homie. Marriage is a very scary thing."

"Babe, leave Shane alone," Alyssa said with a hiss.

"I'm just saying. Out of Cherie, Jessica and April, who knew that April would be the one making it down the aisle? I mean, of course, I did because I hooked them up."

Quita placed her hand on the hip of her satin gown. "I'm about to put you out. He's going through enough."

"Where's my daughter?" he asked the with a raspy voice.

Ashington left the chambers to fetch Miracle from Joyce.

"Brother, you don't have to do this," Quita reminded him. "You're not a punk if you just back out now."

"Bring me my kid."

"Shane—"

"I want my *daughter!*"

Quita flinched. She then took Erykah by the hand and left the chambers altogether. Alyssa followed suit. She didn't want to be around when her brother turned into a beast for an unknown reason. It was more than evident that Shane was making a mistake on his wedding day, yet he didn't want to face it.

"Shane, April's a good girl," Rich announced. He traveled over to the vanity and grabbed a few tissues out of a sitting box, then handed them to his friend. "Your nerves are getting the best of you. All of those thoughts of what could've been is going through your mind. You never listened to me before now, so hopefully, you will this time."

Shane stood, accepting his tissue to wipe his mouth with.

Rich straightened the lapel of his tuxedo jacket as he continued. "You and Cherie would've been beautiful together. You tried, my brotha. You tried. Look at Mandy and me. I loved that girl with everything in me, but we didn't work out. I tried, and we still didn't work. So, I left. That's what you do when shit goes array, and there's nothing that you can do about it. *However…*" Rich stood back to inspect his best friend's attire. "If it ain't April that you want, and you got some fight left in you… go for the kill. It's all or nothing at all." Finally, Rich handed Shane his shiny patent leather dress shoes to put on. "It ain't too late."

———

The music struck up, and April's heart was pounding outside of her chest. As she walked down the aisle, with Rich on her arm to give her away. The only face that she could bring herself to look at was Cherie's. For some reason, Cherie was sitting on her side of the church. She gulped as she passed her, hoping and praying that she would grab the train of her dress to stop her from marrying Shane. It was all too late when she reached the altar.

"Who here gives this man away to this woman?" The pastor asked.

"I do," Rich spoke proudly. He then kissed April's hand before helping her up on the small platform. He took his place behind Shane, massaging his best friend's shoulders.

"You all may be seated," the pastor prompted the guests. "Let us pray over this union."

During prayer, April looked to her side at Cherie, who had her head bowed. Then, she took her eyes to Shane. Were they really going to be stubborn and let them marry? Was neither of them going to give in to the things that they were thinking?

As the pastor read a scripture from the Bible, Shane's gaze fell upon April, yet his peripheral was steady and on Cherie. Was she going to make a move? She sat in the pew as solid as a rock. *She's really over me*, Shane thought. *She doesn't really want me. She's letting me marry the hell out of April right now. Come on, Rie. Say something. Do something. Give me permission to back out of this thing.*

They are this damn stubborn that it doesn't even make any sense, April said to herself. *Look at him, with his sexy dimples and champion's smile. He really wants to be with me for the rest of his life? Is he really mine to claim? Do I really have all of him?*

He better not fuck this up, Cherie thought. You motherfucker. You couldn't act right for me, but you better be a damn good husband for her. Now, hold it together, Rie. Just like that. So steady, baby. It's almost over. You're here for support, not to ruin this moment for him. This is what's best for him. Remember that. Hold your peace.

Baby, please! Shane begged. Save me, dammit! Say something! Do something! I can't let you go, fuck! I don't want to let go!

"If anyone has reason for these two not to wed, speak now or forever hold your peace," the pastor announced.

Shane kept his eyes on April's until hers diverted. She looked over at Cherie on her side of the church. Slowly, April let down her gorgeous bouquet from her chest and took one sloppy step back.

What the hell is she about to do?

TO BE CONTINUED

Readers,

At which point do we stop and surrender? When do we realize that being in love and being broken is like standing in the middle of an avalanche? It's almost like our spirit is dying, and we wish, pray, and hope that our significant other comes along to breathe life into us. They will hold our still-beating hearts in the palms of their hands without so much as acknowledging it. We allow them to— trusting them to keep it safe but dread the thought of them doing something unimaginable with it. When the unthinkable happens, we're stuck in between suffocating and breathing. We have two separate roads to take then. Either we could go north, save ourselves and breathe our own air some sort of way, or we could go south and dive into what was supposed to be familiar territories and trust these seemingly deceitful people all over again. Love isn't easy, and the majority of us understand. However, if we can sustain the pain and put enough trust into it, maybe it will be worth it. But blessed be the broken. From their wounds ooze a beautiful art that can never be reproduced. Thus, I penned *Stuck on You 3: Shane & Cherie's Story* from my experiences and from my wounds. I give you something that we can control— a story of love, hate, and redemption.

Sunny Giovanni

OTHER ROYAL RELEASES FROM SUNNY

Chosen: A Street King's Obsession

Chosen 2: A Street King's Obsession

Chosen 3: A Street King's Obsession

Givana & Slay: A No Questions Asked Love Story

A Forbidden Street King's Love Story

A Forbidden Street King's Love Story 2: Through Hell & High Water

Love & Cocaine: A Savage Love Story

Love & Cocaine 2: For Better or Worse

Stuck on You: Shane & Cherie's Story

Stuck on You 2: Shane & Cherie's Story

Obsessed with a Savage

Caught Between Two Street Kings

Looking for a publishing home?

Royalty Publishing House, Where the Royals reside, is accepting submissions for writers in the urban fiction genre. If you're interested, submit the first 3-4 chapters with your synopsis to submissions@royaltypublishinghouse.com.

Check out our website for more information:

www.royaltypublishinghouse.com.

Text ROYALTY to 42828 to join our mailing list!

To submit a manuscript for our review, email us at
submissions@royaltypublishinghouse.com

Text RPHCHRISTIAN to 22828 for our
CHRISTIAN ROMANCE novels!

Text RPHROMANCE to 22828 for our
INTERRACIAL ROMANCE novels!

"For those who dare to love…"

CONNECT WITH SUNNY!

Twitter & Instagram: @imthatgiovanni

Tumblr: knojokegio.tumblr.com

Google Plus: Sunny Giovanni

Facebook: https://www.facebook.com/thesunnygiovanni/

Get LiT!

Download the LiTeReader app today and enjoy exclusive content, free books, and more

Do You Like CELEBRITY GOSSIP?

Check Out QUEEN DYNASTY!
Visit Our Site: www.thequeendynasty.com